THE DISAPPEARANCE

Sharon!
Thank you! :-)
Enjoy!

Lisa Hodorovych

THE DISAPPEARANCE

Lisa Hodorovych

Quoth the Writer, L.L.C.
Whippany, NJ

Quoth the Writer

Where a writer's dreams become a published reality.

Quoth the Writer, L.L.C.

Publication Production Company

Whippany, NJ 07981

qtwpublishing@gmail.com

www.quoththewriter.com

Cover Design by Mark Bailey

ISBN (paperback): 978-0-578-36534-3

ISBN (eBook): 978-0-578-36535-0

First Edition, September 2020; Second Edition, February 2022

Printed in the United States of America

To my rock, my support system, my favorite, my everything! I love you so much, John! Thank you for always believing in me and pushing me! Here's to many more!

Note from Author, Lisa Hodorovych

Hello and welcome to the *second edition* of my book, my baby, *The Disappearance.*

It was first published in September of 2020 by Serial Writer Productions. Now, in February of 2022, it is being re-released under my publication, Quoth the Writer, L.L.C., with a new cover and some revisions.

Enjoy!

You'll notice there are a few weeks, a couple of months, and even a few months missing between these journal entries. That's because I either didn't have time to write them (lovely work) or nothing really interesting happened to warrant an entry. Also, as I wrote these entries, I might've accidentally omitted some things. This was a traumatic time for me, and I tried to record everything to the best of my abilities. If something is missing, it might be because I completely forgot about it, or I repressed it.

~Ashlynn Amuso

AUGUST 31st

This day is always the saddest for me because it's the last day of vacation. Tomorrow my brother, Glen, my besties, Roman and Kaden, and I resume work. Yes, we've been home for a couple of days now, but I'm still in vacation mode. I still feel like I'm in the Caribbean and I have the burn to prove it.

Kaden and Roman came over mine and Glen's apartment around six for dinner. After eating, I immediately asked, "So who's turn is it to choose for next year?"

Kaden reacted, "Ash, we just got back. How about we go back to work first before we start planning our next vacation?"

"True, but this is my favorite time of the year!" I exclaimed.

Glen looked at me confused. "I thought Halloween was your favorite time of the year?"

I rolled my eyes. "Okay, so it's Halloween first and our vacation a close second, but still. I'm ready for our next one," I whined like a child.

"Damn, Ash. You make it sound like you have the world's worst job. Do we really make things that difficult for you?" Roman asked, sarcastically.

Even though I knew he was being his usual asshole self, I still kind of felt bad. "No, not at all. Don't get me wrong guys, I love my job. I love working for *Replay* and I love working with you guys, but when all we do is work – and I mean literally breathing it, sweating it, and bleeding it like that accident that Glen had…"

They all cringed, remembering that fateful day. Glen said, "I still have the scar from that damn fall," as he showed us his arm.

About a year or two into working at *Replay* (an entertainment company based in New York) – so about three or four years ago now – Glen, who helps build all the sets, climbed up a scaffolding. But he wasn't paying attention to where he was placing his feet, missed a step, and fell. Thankfully, he wasn't seriously injured. He walked away with some bumps, bruises, and a fractured arm. Our boss, Mr. Schneider, agreed he was very lucky. He saw the whole thing happen and told me if he fell differently, he could've possibly banged his head on the stage and died.

I retorted, "Yeah, well being the one to call home was no picnic. I have a mental scar from calling our parents and saying, 'Hey, Mom. Hi, Dad. Um…don't be alarmed, but Glen was in an accident.' Mom freaked out and blamed *me* for not watching over you."

Glen laughed so hard. "I thought that was great! I was the one not paying attention and you're the one getting yelled at!"

I sneered at him. "Yeah, having a baby brother is a pain in the ass because apparently you're responsible for them, even when they're turning thirty in like two years."

"Yeah, but who's thirty already?"

I growled, "Thanks for the reminder, jerk."

The boys laughed. I pointed to Roman and Kaden. "The both of you are older than me so shut it."

As I now laughed, Roman remarked, "Yeah, but only by a year, Ash."

"I know, I'm just busting." I got up to put dishes into the sink. "So like I was saying, I do love my job, but when we work non-stop for however many days out of the year and then we get this two-month break from July till September, it's just…magical."

Kaden agreed, "We do work ourselves overtime for this two-month break, so we definitely deserve it." He thought for a second. "Well, Roman picked first. That was when we went to Mexico."

Roman interrupted him, "Which reminds me, I need to get back there. I got a couple of girls waiting for me."

"And you wonder why I never dated you," I said.

"What?! I'm irresistible, baby," he replied with a wink.

I acted like I was about to vomit. Kaden continued, "Anyway, Glen was second and we went to Florida to visit your parents and this time I picked the Caribbean, so it looks like it's your turn, Ash."

"Yes!" I jumped up and down, dancing around my kitchen like my favorite song just came on the radio.

"I guess you know where we're going next year," Kaden chuckled.

"Yup! I know the perfect place."

JUNE 1ˢᵗ

I cannot wait!

Kaden, Roman, Glen and I have been working incessantly for the past nine months leading up to this. We are one month away from vaca. This time, I picked where we were going and to me it's paradise. We're going to Lake Minnetaha, Washington. It is about a half hour from Olympia and about two hours from Seattle. The best way I can describe it: it's a place of tranquility and relaxation.

My parents bought a cabin in the middle of a sparse, but lush green forest surrounded by Douglas firs, western red cedars, and western hemlocks...or at least that's what I found in my research. All I know is if any of those trees fell, no matter where in the world you are, you would know it.

There aren't too many animals around as there's a county law for animal control, which made the cabin safe. Thankfully, the animals weren't killed, just relocated. Some went to national parks and some to different areas in Washington. There's a strict law against hunting in Amitola Township, which consists of Lake Minnetaha and other surrounding towns. Again, they wanted to make it a peaceful place. What better way to do so then by outlawing hunting and moving the animals that would be preyed upon to a safe and secure location?

The "backyard" faces a small hill that goes into a valley where there are no trees, just some grass and twigs among other debris. The lake itself is about a mile long and wide, this perfect circle in the middle of nowhere. It's surrounded by cabins, but they aren't stacked on top of each other. Instead, they're spread apart, so we have some neighbors, but it still feels secluded. Another reason why my parents fell in love with it. The lake is to the right of the cabin, about ten feet away. Lastly, there's a small town called Nonoma about five minutes away by car.

All of this was exactly why I wanted to take the boys there this year for our vacation. I was ecstatic when I told them about the cabin last year and they all immediately agreed. Glen even said, "When it was your turn, I hoped you would say the cabin."

See, Glen and I started working at *Replay* about five years ago. One of the big perks of working there is our "summer vacation". Mr. Schneider, who is the owner and, again, our boss, decided – maybe three years after he opened its doors – that his employees deserved some time off. With everything going so well, he was able to close the company down for two months in July and August. He wanted to make sure everyone could enjoy the warm weather, whether they stayed in the States, went to Europe, or wherever.

You need to understand though that *Replay* is open seven days a week. We, the employees, work from about eight in the morning until about midnight every single day. We prepare everything in the a.m. and then in the evening is when people start filing in to watch the shows. Every single day we're making close to five grand between the tickets, the food, and the merchandise we sell. Sometimes it's more and sometimes it's less, but it's all amazing; especially for a small company.

I will never forget when Teddy, who was the sweetest man and worked for *Replay* for fifteen years before retiring last year, once told me, "You know, I thought Mr. Schneider was absolutely insane when he announced his vacation plan for us. I just couldn't imagine us being busy after being closed for two months, even though July and August were kind of our slower months. But I was sorely mistaken. Thank God, Mr. Schneider is a savvy businessman."

So anyway, like I was saying, Glen and I started about five years ago with Roman and Kaden following our trails not too long afterward. We all immediately became friends. We missed the first summer vacation together but decided the following year we would do every single one jointly. We haven't looked back since.

JULY 1st

I barely got any sleep last night I was so damn excited! Today is the day! Let summer vacation begin!

<u>Continued:</u>

After about a six-hour plane ride and an hour and a half car ride, we arrived at my second home, at one of my favorite places in the world: my family's cabin in Lake Minnetaha, WA.

The second we parked the car and stepped out it was like entering a whole new world. We had gone from the hustle and bustle of New York to the peace and quiet of Washington. Kaden and Roman felt a little out of their element, though. They've never been somewhere so secluded.

"Don't you worry, guys," I said. "It'll feel like home in no time."

JULY 4th

Today, Roman and Kaden finally felt a little more relaxed as we celebrated the Fourth of July. We started out with a hike around the backyard. They couldn't believe the land, the forest that surrounded the cabin. When I told them about the valley just over the hill, they wanted to check it out. Once we reached the top and looked down into it, Roman and Kaden just stared in awe, stunned that this bare land was encompassed by a lush forest. They questioned, "How could this be?"

I told them of a story, a myth from a local Native American tribe that has been passed down from generation to generation and from tribe to tribe. It's about how two beings created the world, so they could have a home. They created the mountains, the oceans, and the forests; all these different places they could live in depending on where they wanted to be. But after some time, they started feeling lonely. They constructed this beautiful world, but they were the only ones seeing it. They wanted to share it with others, so they created different creatures. However, these creatures were a bunch of troublemakers: burning the forests they worked so hard on, polluting the water with their filth. This angered the creators, so they produced a massive flood to destroy them. After that flood, certain parts of the Earth couldn't grow anymore with this valley being one of them.

I also told them the reason this area is called Amitola

Township is because after the flood, the creators made a beautiful rainbow rise above it to signify a new beginning; an amitola, as the Native Americans call it.

"Wow. That's so beautiful, Ashlynn," Kaden said.

Of course, Roman had a different response. "Wow. That's so...boring."

"Really, dude!" I exclaimed.

"Well, if you said a meteor came down and made this massive hole that would be so much cooler."

I rolled my eyes and sighed angrily. "I'm walking away before I punch you in your balls."

"Aw, that dirty talk, girl. What did I tell you about that?"

I continued walking as I shook my head and chuckled. He can be such an asshole, but God help me I love him. Him and Kaden are the older brothers I never had, but kind of wanted. It's nice to have someone to look up to, like Glen has with me, even if one of them is a prick.

After the hike, we took a dip in the lake to cool off. By twelve o'clock, Roman was asking where the drinks were. Glen said, "Dude, it's only noon."

"Yeah, but it's five o'clock somewhere, especially today."

It took us a moment before realizing, "Holy shit, he's right!"

He announced, "Damn, right! Let the drinking begin!"

We finished the day by watching movies and enjoying some barbeque.

JULY 9th

The last couple of days have been great. Our morning ritual has become eating breakfast, going out for a hike in the backyard, going for a swim in the lake, washing up, and doing whatever the rest of the day brings our way. Today, however, once we got cleaned up, Glen and I had a "discussion".

"Do you think it's time we show them?" I asked.

"Kaden, yeah. Roman, not so much."

Kaden looked at us. "Show us what?"

I joked, "Yeah, you're right. I think Roman might be a little too much for it."

Roman got somewhat irritated. "What the hell are you guys talking about? I'm perfect for whatever this is."

We all laughed. I said, "So, Glen and I want to show you this small town that's maybe five minutes away from here called Nonoma. It's literally our home away from home. We would always go there to get away from our parents when we just wanted some time to ourselves. It's an amazing town."

The inquisitive one, Kaden, asked, "Well, what's in it? What's it like?"

"Honestly, the best way I can describe it is…remember that extremely small town in the first *Cars* movie. Radiator Springs I think it was called."

They nodded.

"Well, it's kind of like that. Just this little strip that contains a few stores in it, a restaurant or two, the sheriff's department, and a movie theater. Nobody actually lives in the town, except for the sheriff who has an apartment above the jailhouse. Everyone lives in neighboring towns like Lake Minnetaha."

"So, what is it mainly for then?"

"It's kind of like a tourist attraction. Just a place for people who are either traveling up to Seattle, the national parks, or to Olympia to stop, stretch their legs, grab something to eat or drink…"

That's when Roman perked up. "Drink?!"

I shook my head. "Yes, you alci. There is a bar in this town."

"Perfect! Now we can get our party on!" He jumped out of his seat and rushed for the door.

"Oh my gosh, can you wait a second? Glen and I are not done with our spiel."

Roman stopped dead in his tracks and turned toward us. "Well, hurry up. I got drinks to drink and girls to meet."

"Good Lord, you are such a pain. Anyway," I continued, "it's great for passersby, but it's great for locals as well. It has a grocery store, a clothing store, and a movie theater, which actually shows some pretty awesome movies."

Glen was getting all excited because he couldn't wait for me to make this one particular announcement. He shouted, "Like what, Ash? Like what?"

I exclaimed, "Like the new *Avengers* movie! It actually just came out today. I say let's go grab some lunch, watch the movie, grab a drink afterwards, and see where the rest of the night takes us."

Kaden said, "Watch out, Ash. Your planner is showing."

I laughed. "Sorry, I can't help it. It's a part of me."

He continued, "Well, I'm in love with the idea. Are we all ready to go?"

Glen and I ecstatically proclaimed, "Yes!" while Roman answered, "I've been ready, but didn't that movie come out like last month?"

"Yeah, so what?" I replied.

"And it's not Friday. Why do they have movies coming out during the week?"

"Because they do things differently around here. God, since when did you become Kaden and start asking so many questions?"

"Hey. I resemble that remark," Kaden replied.

We all laughed. Roman then realized, "So that's why when we all wanted to go to the opening night, you said, 'No.' You were planning this all along."

I shrugged. "Maybe."

We all laughed again as we grabbed our stuff and headed over to the small and quaint town of Nonoma.

****

Both Roman and Kaden instantly fell in love with the town.

Kaden said it kind of reminded him of home. It wasn't as big or as crazy as New York, but it still had some tourists and a natural wonder about it. Roman asked, "Why the hell didn't we come here on the Fourth? I bet this place was hopping."

"Because the whole town shuts down on holidays, so people can celebrate with their family and friends," I explained.

"What? That's lame!"

I glared at him. "Seriously! Not every town is a party

town, Roman!"

"It is when I'm in it," he replied with so much smug.

After grabbing some food at the pizzeria – which we all agreed was nothing like having a slice in New York – we went to see the movie. I cried like a baby toward the end. As we walked out of the theater, Kaden's arm wrapped around my shoulders, I said, "Man, I can't wait for the next one. Hopefully, I don't cry at the end of it."

Roman said, "You should've sat next to me, hon. You know I'm very good at comforting others."

"Yeah, I'm sure you would've really 'comforted' me."

He winked at me.

"Now, stupid question, who's ready for a drink?"

"Girl, I thought you would never ask," Roman said. "Then follow me."

We walked over to The Lake's Drinking Hole, a hole in the wall bar with pool tables, a shuffleboard, and a dart board. It hosts game nights every Wednesday, which I'm sure once Roman hears, we'll be back every Wednesday to play. It's where Glen and I had our first drinks when we were…well…we were old enough to have one with our parents. And since we became good friends with the owner, he was totally fine with it as long as our parents were around. If they weren't, he wouldn't give us a drink until we were of age. And when we turned 21, we both had some awesome parties!

Walking in, I checked to see if the sheriff was sitting in his usual spot. He was. He claimed a table off to the corner near the back of the bar where he wouldn't be bothered. I nudged Kaden and whispered, "That's," pointing to him, "Sheriff MacReedy."

"That's the notorious sheriff you've been talking about."

I nodded.

Roman then pulled into us with Glen. "What are we talking about?"

I chuckled. "I was telling Kaden that's the sheriff I've been telling you guys about."

Roman looked over and yelled, "Sheriff MacReedy!"

He – along with everyone else in the bar – immediately turned toward us. We all grabbed him and said, "Shut the fuck up! What the hell is wrong with you?"

Thank God the sheriff is an easygoing guy. He yelled back, "Hey, you! I don't know you, but let's have a drink!" He got up and walked over to us.

Sheriff MacReedy is a sweet, older man (in his 60's) from Texas. He has that "southern charm" about him. He always calls me darlin', but the best part about him…he always had a beer in his hand, whether he was on the clock or not.

Roman said to us, "I love this guy!"

"I told you he's the coolest."

As he walked up to us, the sheriff noticed me. "Ashlynn?"

I waved. "Hi, Sheriff."

He smiled. "Oh, Ms. Ashlynn," he gave me a big, bear hug, "it's so good to see you, darlin'."

I reciprocated. "It's so good to see you, too, Sheriff."

"I was wondering when you were going to make a trip up to my town."

"Yeah, sorry about that. We took longer than I thought because of these two," referring to Roman and Kaden.

"They took a little longer to get used to the change."

He let out a boisterous laugh. "Too quiet for you gents."

Roman replied, "Well, I'm used to more of a party atmosphere."

"I can tell. You must be…," he looked over at me.

I said, "Roman."

"Yes. Ms. Ashlynn told me all about you and…," he panned over to Kaden.

"Oh, I'm sorry, sir. I'm Kaden," he replied as he stuck out his hand to properly greet the sheriff.

"Sir?! Wow!" Sheriff MacReedy shook his hand. "It's not too often you get 'sir' from a young man. Ashlynn was right about you; you are the respectable one."

Roman added, "I meant to call you 'sir'. I just got a little excited to finally meet you."

The sheriff laughed again. "Don't worry, son. I'm not going to arrest you for not calling me 'sir'." Then he turned to my brother. "And Glen, my boy, how are you? Staying out of trouble?"

Glen replied, "The best I can, sir."

"That a boy," he said as he patted Glen on the back. He continued, "So I guess y'all learned about me just as much as I learned about you."

"Well, you know, Sheriff, as the 'planner' of this group, I wanted to make sure everyone was prepared," I responded.

From there we sat down with him. We had drink after drink as he told us story after story of his time being a sheriff in Texas.

JULY 10th

This morning…well…fucking sucked. I wasn't as sick as the others were, but I definitely had a nasty headache and threw up at least twice. Glen, Roman, and Kaden I lost count after five. Good thing we had Gatorade in the cabin for just the occasion. That's pretty much all we had and maybe some crackers. We moved into the living room to watch TV and that's where we stayed the entire day. Even for dinner, as we started to feel better, we ate toast. We weren't going to push our stomachs.

Sheriff MacReedy was kind enough to call and check in on us. "I told y'all wouldn't be able to keep up with me," he jested.

"How the hell are you not hungover, Sheriff?" I asked lying on the couch, cradling my Gatorade like it was a baby.

"Years of practice. And I'm a Texan. It's in our blood to be immune to alcohol like the Russians and the Irish."

"Shit. Well, I'm not from Texas, nor do I have Russian or Irish blood in my veins, so I guess I'll just have to keep on 'practicing' to be as good as you."

He laughed. "Ms. Ashlynn, if you do that, we might be rushing you to the hospital fairly often to get your stomach pumped."

"Yeah, no, I'm good."

We both laughed. He then asked, "So will I be seeing y'all at the bar tomorrow night for game night?"

"Oh, definitely. Roman could be on his deathbed and he would get up to go to game night."

"You're damn right I would," he said from the neighboring couch.

"Good. Continue drinking the Gatorade, but make sure y'all get water in you as well and I will see y'all tomorrow."

"We will. Thanks, Sheriff."

"You're welcome, darlin'. Feel better."

For the first time since getting here, we all went to bed before midnight.

JULY 23rd

The past couple of weeks have been crazy yet calming. Instantly, Nonoma became our "hangout." We went there for groceries (where I think Kaden met someone), to catch a movie, shop around, and, of course, have a drink, which was always with Sheriff MacReedy. Shockingly, Roman and the sheriff became best friends. I thought they would be mortal enemies because of the way he can be, but they bonded over alcohol, which I was very happy about. At least I didn't have to worry about bailing him out of jail every time we were in town.

However, it wasn't just Roman who bonded with the sheriff; Glen and Kaden did as well. Well, Glen always had a friendship with the sheriff, but I feel like it's gotten stronger while on this trip. They even nicknamed him "Batman" because of the stories he told from when he was a sheriff in Texas. How every minute of every day he was running around fighting crime.

"So then what brought you to Lake Minnetaha, Sheriff?" Kaden inquired one night.

"I used to vacation up here with my late wife, Meredith. I have so many great memories here with her and after almost thirty years on the force, I decided to retire and move here."

I had to ask. "What happened to your wife, Sheriff? You always talk about her, but why is she not with us today?"

"She passed from cancer."

My heart sank. I felt horrible for bringing it up. "I'm so sorry, Sheriff. She was a lucky woman to have you in her life."

He blushed and grabbed my hand. "Aw, thanks, darlin'. I was truly the lucky one, though."

Then Roman did something amazing. He held up his bottle of beer and said, "To Meredith."

We all followed suit. I was pleasantly surprised. Every so often Roman shows off his softer side.

The sheriff went on to tell us that when he moved here, the township of Amitola – which includes Lake Minnetaha and Nonoma – was coincidently looking for a sheriff, so he took the job. He told us, "I still feel like I'm retired, though, because there's never anything going on. It's so much quieter compared to Texas and yet I still get paid. I get paid to do nothing and I live in a beautiful house for free. What more could you ask for?"

Where he lives is truly beautiful. It's a renovated Victorian courthouse – I think it was originally built in the late 1800s, early 1900s – where the downstairs area is his office with jail cells, and the upstairs area is his living quarters.

That same night, the sheriff and I were talking while the boys were playing darts. I said to him, "You know, Sheriff, if I didn't have my eye on someone else, I would totally go out with you."

"Aw, Ms. Ashlynn. You're just saying that."

"No, honestly. You're a nice guy with a heart of gold. Like I said before, any woman would be lucky to have you in their life."

He gave me a peck on the cheek. "Thank you, darlin'.

That means a lot to me."

"You're welcome. If you don't mind me asking, how long were you and Mrs. MacReedy together?"

"We were about to celebrate our 35th anniversary when she passed."

I grew sadder. "I'm so…"

"No, no, please. Let's not make this seem so sad. She's in a better place with no more pain."

I nodded. "You're right. And I'm guessing there hasn't been any others since her."

"Nope. She was my first and only."

"Aw," I said as I placed my hands over my heart. I love stories of true love between two people.

Then the sheriff asked, "So, who's the guy you have your eyes on? Wait…let me guess. Is it Kaden?"

"Nope," I said as I took a swig of my beer

He was shocked. "Really? But the way you two are…"

I put my bottle of beer down and stopped him before he said anymore. "Yeah, trust me everybody has thought the exact same thing, but…he's gay."

His eyes bugged out of his head and his mouth dropped to the floor. "He's what?!"

"Yup. He came out to me a year after we started working together."

"So…wait…what…how…"

Before his head exploded, I explained, "He came out to his parents, but they didn't exactly 'approve', so they kicked him out. That's when he moved to New York and started to work for *Replay*. He tried to hide it, thinking everybody was going to be like his parents. He even asked me out on a date, but I turned him down. After some time, he came out to me.

That's when he realized that we're *nothing* like his parents and came out to everyone. We've been best friends ever since."

He was still stunned but understood.

****

To top everything off, last Sunday we started going on random car rides throughout the week to take in the beauty of Washington. It was (shocker) Kaden's idea to do something different other than hiking or swimming or drinking. Each time we went out, we took a different route to see what was around the area. We also made pit stops at random locations to take in the natural world.

However, it was on today's ride that we took a left instead of a right down this one road because, as Kaden said, "Why the hell not?"

While driving, we saw this white, boxed building. It was up a hill and behind some trees. There were no signs indicating what it was, just a three-story building in the middle of nowhere. We, of course, turned around, pulled over, and got out to take a closer look at it. I said to Glen, "Do you remember ever seeing something like this?"

He shook his head. "Nope, but I also don't remember ever coming down this way. We've always made the right."

"True. Mom and Dad aren't exactly the exploring type. If they know one way to get somewhere, that's the way they'll always go."

"Exactly."

I joked, "And it's like they're trying to hide it, but, at the same time, say, 'Hey, we're over here!' The building looks newer, too. I mean, I know it's been a few years since we've been here, but I don't remember Mom and Dad mentioning anything being built. Do you?"

He again shook his head.

We continued staring at it for a little while longer, perplexed that something like that was placed in such a beautiful area. Then Roman said, "I dare one of you to go up there."

Now we all shook our heads.

"Chickens!"

I replied, "First of all, do you not see that fence with signs that say, 'Do Not Trespass'?"

"So, what? You can climb over that fence."

"Yeah, and what if you get caught?!"

"That's easy, I won't."

"So then why don't you go up there?"

He thought about it for a second. "Nah, not feeling so limber today."

We all gave him shit for that. We stood around a little while longer until I said, "Can we go guys? This place is starting to give me the creeps."

They all agreed, and we left. Before I got back into the car, I thought I heard a faint sound. I thought I heard someone screaming. I gasped. "Holy shit! Did you guys hear that?"

"Hear what?" they asked in unison.

"Shush, listen. I thought I heard someone screaming."

We stood silent for a moment, staring at the building, but heard nothing. "Maybe it was just my imagination."

"Yeah, horror girl," Roman joked.

As we drove, we talked about the building. Kaden asked, "What if they're doing some secret tests there?"

"And you guys say I watch too many horror movies," I retorted.

"No but seriously, guys. Maybe one day we should go

check it out," Kaden stated.

Roman chimed in, "Well, I wanted to do that now, but you guys were too chicken shit to do so."

We all yelled, "Shut up, Roman!"

He mumbled, "Just saying."

I, then, said, "Well, maybe you can ask Charlie at the grocery store. See if he knows anything."

Roman and Glen chuckled while Kaden blushed. "If I get a date with him, maybe I will."

Glen retorted, "Not *if*, dude, *when*!"

Kaden grinned and replied, "Yes, *when* I get a date…"

We all hooted and hollered.

Then I tried to be the sensible one in the group. "In all seriousness, guys, there was that 'Do Not Trespass' sign on the fence. I don't know about you, but we have a little over a month left of our vacation and I would like to spend it *not* in a jail cell."

They all agreed. Although, I was just as curious about it as they were.

JULY 30ᵗʰ

This past week has been weird. After seeing the building, it was all we talked about. Like when people talk about the most recent episode of a popular TV show. Now that I think about it, I still don't understand why we were so consumed by that building. We even told Sheriff MacReedy about it during game night. When Roman mentioned he wanted to jump the fence and check it out, the sheriff became infuriated. He yelled, "Don't you dare go near that place! It's not safe! You go anywhere near it, and I will arrest you!"

That, of course, made Roman want to go check it out even more. We almost had to tie him down to a chair to make sure he didn't. However, two nights later – so this past Friday – I went to use the restroom at the bar and when I went back to the boys, they seemed…different. Roman was practically jumping out of his seat while Kaden and Glen looked like they were about to kill him. I asked, "Oh, shit! What the hell did you do now, Roman?"

He scowled at me. "Why do you always think I did something wrong?" I just folded my arms and glared at him. "Yeah, you're right. But don't worry about it, hon. We'll tell you about it later."

I looked at Glen and Kaden. "Ah, okay." I was extremely confused.

****

This past weekend was a little tense. We still went out, we still had fun, but I felt like there was this tension between the boys.

Whenever I asked them about it, they would just say, "It's nothing. Don't worry about it."

Then when I woke up this morning, the boys were gone. I was baffled. I checked every room at least twice. I checked the lake. I walked around the backyard screaming their names. I tried calling them with no answer. I tried texting them with no answer until finally at 5:15 p.m. Kaden responded with, "I'm so sorry, Ash. We were taking a survey. We'll be back in a little bit."

A survey? What survey did you take that made you gone all day? I thought.

About ten minutes later they were back. They walked in gingerly while I ran up to them, hugging them so tight they couldn't breathe. "Oh my gosh, where were you guys? Why didn't you tell me? Why didn't you invite me?"

Kaden said, "Why do I have a funny feeling the most important question to answer right now is why you weren't invited?"

"Damn right!"

We all laughed, but the boys' laughs were more contained. They looked to be in so much pain.

"But seriously, guys, where did you go? What happened? Why didn't you leave a note or tell me you were leaving so early? I was worried sick about you."

"I think the twenty million text messages you left us was a good indication of that," Roman replied.

"Would you rather none?"

"One would've been enough."

I frowned. "I severely can't with you right now, Roman. So, is anyone going to give me a serious answer?"

"Honestly, we forgot," Glen answered while shrugging.

"Okay, but why are you guys beating around the bush and not telling me the full truth?"

"Maybe because you don't need to fucking know," Roman responded, harshly.

I turned to him seething. "Excuse me?!" I was ready to pounce on him and rip him apart.

Kaden stepped in between us and said, "What Roman means is it's nothing to really worry about, hon. We just had a long day, and we want to get some rest."

I backed off. I was so hurt and so pissed off. I thought, *What are they hiding from me? Why won't they tell me what they did today?*

But I still helped them relax and made some dinner before we sat down to watch TV and head to bed.

AUGUST 2nd

The last several days have been difficult to say the least. Glen, Roman, and Kaden continued to wake up before me and leave. They started writing notes that simply read, "Went into Nonoma. Be back later." Then after a full day had passed, they would return exhausted and in pain.

I would question them, trying to figure out what was going on, but they incessantly replied with, "Nothing, don't worry about it." From there, I didn't want to push since they were so worn out and achy. I didn't want to stress them out any further.

This morning, however, I decided to set an alarm to wake up as early as possible. As it went off, I heard them walking around and whispering. I immediately popped out of bed, walked out and said, "Morning. Off to Nonoma?"

They stopped, stared at me, and looked at each other with shock and fear in their eyes. They didn't say a word, but their eyes screamed, "Oh, shit! What do we do?"

I coaxed them, "Guys, come on! What's going on?!"

Roman stepped forward and protested, "Ash, it's none of your business, so stop questioning us about it!"

I became enraged. "I'm sorry, did you just say it's none of my business? You guys are my fucking brothers! You disappear, leaving me alone all day with no car so I can't go anywhere..."

Roman retorted, "You can call an Uber."

"Really, Roman?! You think they have fucking Uber around here?"

He shrugged.

"That's not the point, though. The point is you come back exhausted and in pain. I'm showing genuine concern for you and it's none of my fucking business."

They stared at the floor with no response. "Fine, then go!" I walked away from them. "Have fun at your fucking pow wow!"

They left as I stood in the living room looking out to the forest and hill, breathing deeply to calm down. It didn't take me long, though, to realize I was wrong in what I said. I got dressed and waited for them to come back, so I could help them. The second they walked in, later in the evening, I took care of them, apologizing profusely for my behavior. "You guys know I'm an Italian New Yorker. It's in my blood to be a nasty bitch sometimes."

While preparing for bed, Kaden and I went outside to talk, something we haven't done in quite some time – actually since they started leaving. We always told each other everything, so I was hoping he would open up to me. When I asked him the same question I have been, he stuttered, "We've been going into Nonoma to do some stuff."

"Okay, what stuff?"

"I can't say."

Trying to stay calm, I replied, "What do you mean you 'can't say'?"

"I…I was sworn to secrecy."

My heart skipped a beat. "What do you mean, Kaden? You're starting to scare me."

He gently grabbed my hand. "And I don't mean to scare

you, hon. It's just…that's all I can say. I'm sorry."

Not too long after, he decided we should get some sleep. We gave each other a hug. He whispered to me, "Please know that I am truly sorry and that I love you." He then let go of me and went back into the cabin.

I watched him, wondering what the hell just happened. All that ran through my mind as I tried to get some sleep was, *I'm going to get to the bottom of this, even if it kills me!*

AUGUST 3rd

When I woke up this morning, I did my "new" routine of checking to see if the boys left for the day or not. I was pleasantly surprised to see they were all still sleeping. I silently screamed and jumped around. I thought, *Today is going to be a great day!*

While they continued to sleep, I decided to surprise them with an awesome breakfast. I made pancakes, waffles, eggs…you name it, I probably made it. Slowly, each one crept out of their little caves to see what was going on. Glen was the first, which didn't surprise me. He has the appetite of a sumo wrestler, but not the body of one. I have no freaking clue where he packs it. "What's that smell?" he exclaimed. "It's delicious!"

"That would be the most amazing breakfast that your most amazing sister is cooking up for you. And Roman and Kaden."

He snapped his fingers. "Oh man, I was hoping this would all be for me."

I laughed.

Not too long after, Roman and Kaden came out absolutely stunned at what I did. Kaden asked, "What's this for, hon?"

"Because I feel bad for the way I've been treating you guys. I've been giving you a hard time this week and with you guys being here when you're usually gone, I figured I would treat you to a nice breakfast."

They all came over to give me a kiss on the cheek, except for Roman who tried for my lips. I grabbed my spatula and said, "Hey. I have a spatula and I know how to use it."

He laughed. "Please, tease me with a good time, girl."

I spanked him lightly with it.

As we stuffed our faces with food, we talked, we laughed, we had a good ol' time. It was like nothing ever happened, until I asked, "So, does this mean you guys are all done with whatever you were doing?"

They stopped eating and looked at each other. Whatever happiness that was on their faces instantly depleted. They became rigid and looked like they were about to be sick. That's when the fun ended. One-by-one, they left the table saying, "Thanks, Ash, but I'm not hungry." I sat at the table ready to burst into tears. *What did I say?* I thought. *We were just having a great time.*

While cleaning, the boys came out of their rooms with their bags. I stared at them. My heart sank. I said, "Uh, guys, by my calculations we still have about four weeks left of our vacation. Why are your bags packed now?"

Kaden looked at me with sad eyes. "I'm sorry, Ash, but we have to go."

I became extremely concerned. I came around the counter and said, "What do you mean? Did something happen at *Replay*? Is Mr. Schneider okay?"

Mr. Schneider is an older gentleman who treats everyone with a lot of love and respect. If anything ever happened to him, I would be devastated.

"No, we're not going back to New York. We're just…going away," Kaden retorted with agitation.

I grabbed ahold of his arm. "Then to where, Kaden? And for how long? Please, talk to me."

He touched my hand. "I'm sorry, Ashlynn, but that's all I can say."

I let go of him. *God damn it, Kaden!*

I looked at Roman and Glen. "Roman?" He just looked down and said nothing. "Glen?"

He came over to me, gently gripped my shoulders, and apologized. "I'm so sorry, Ash, but we can't say anything. We were…"

"Sworn to secrecy, I know!"

We stood around in silence for a moment. My anger became sadness. I started to cry. "But you guys are my brothers; especially you, Glen. You're my own flesh and blood. You can't even tell me where you're going or what's going on? You're just going to leave me here alone?"

Kaden started, "Some things must be kept unknown to pro…"

"Oh, don't give me your philosophical bullshit right now, Kaden."

They all felt horrible. They tried to give me a hug before leaving, but I turned away. Between being pissed off and hurt, I couldn't even look at them.

As Glen walked away, he said, "Please don't tell Mom and Dad."

Through clenched teeth, I replied, "No guarantees."

Right before he walked out the door, Kaden turned to me and said, "Know we'll be watching over you, hon."

That was it. They were gone.

I fell to the floor crying hysterically. Between being mad at them for leaving me and at myself for the way I acted, I couldn't help but cry. All I thought was, *I'm all alone! My brothers have left me! How could they have left me?!*

The way I saw it, our perfect vacation was over.

****

It took me some time to regain my composure after they left. While an occasional tear flowed down my cheek, I stomped around the cabin, furious at what happened. I wanted to punch a hole into the wall.

As the sun began to set, I went out for a swim. I knew it was going to be the only thing that would help me calm down other than drinking myself into a coma. (Yes, I realize that would've been stupid!) However, as I walked outside, I noticed our rental car was still in the driveway. "What the fuck?"

I was extremely confused.

I walked back inside and back out thinking I was maybe seeing things. It was still there. I walked over to it and touched it. It was real. I pinched myself. I wasn't dreaming. "They didn't take the car? Why didn't they take the car?" I was baffled. "Now I really need that swim."

After doing several laps, I sat at the edge of the lake letting the water roll onto my feet. That's when I finally felt levelheaded. I said to myself, "Wow, Ash! They tried to say goodbye to you, and you just gave them the cold shoulder. You are such a bitch! Now only God knows when you'll see them again. You better call them and apologize."

I ran back to the cabin, immediately grabbed my phone, and tried to call Kaden, but his phone went straight to voicemail. The same thing happened with Glen and Roman. I tried a couple more times before going to bed, but the same thing happened.

As I laid in bed, my mind raced. I couldn't sleep. I still felt horrible for what I did and was so concerned. They never called me back or texted me. "Why is this happening?" I said out loud. "This is our fun time. Our time away from the craziness and the drama. Yes, there are times Roman causes some of the drama, but still. The past three years have been great."

I continued staring at the ceiling, thinking, when I said, "This is my fault. Coming to Lake Minnetaha was my idea. Whatever happens to them is on me."

AUGUST 4th

All I did today was continue calling and texting the boys. Unfortunately, I still got no answer. Whenever I called, it went straight to voicemail. I texted each of them at least ten times; possibly more. At times my messages were mean, but then I apologized, hoping I would get an answer back. Still nothing.

I guess tomorrow is another day.

AUGUST 7th

For the past two days, all I have been doing is calling and texting the boys with no answers. My anger has become concern. My concern has become fear. I haven't been eating. I haven't been sleeping. I have stayed at the cabin hoping they'll come back, but nothing.

This morning, after what seemed like the one-hundredth attempt, I finally decided I had to go searching for them. "I'm not going to leave until I find them! They never left me intentionally, so I am not going to leave them!"

Before I began my search, I contemplated calling Mr. Schneider to extend my vacation, but then realized, *I should be able to find them within the next three and a half weeks. Why worry him?*

Just as I was about to leave to go see Sheriff MacReedy to file a missing persons' report, my phone rang. It was my mother. "Shit!"

I answered, trying to sound happy, "Hey, Mom!"

"Hi, sweetheart! How's everything going?"

"Great!" *God, I hate lying to her!*

"Good. I'm sorry I haven't called in a few days. Dad and I have been doing a lot of work around the house, so we decided to, what do you kids call it? 'Chillax'?"

I palmed my forehead. "Or you can just say you and Dad have been resting, Mom."

"Then I wouldn't be considered the cool mom."

We laughed. Even with her kids being in their late twenties and early thirties, my mom still had to be the "cool mom." She continued, "So, how's everything going? How are the boys?"

"They're, uh, fine. We're all doing good, thankfully," as I lied again through my goddamn teeth.

"Good, sweetie. What have you guys been up to? I haven't talked to you in like forever."

Oh, god, Mom! "Nothing much. Just the usual."

"Is Roman staying out of trouble?"

"Define 'staying out of'?"

My mom began to worry, "What? What do you mean? Is he okay?"

I chuckled. "Yes, Mom. He's fine. I was just kidding." "Ah," she laughed. "Now I get it."

From day one, my mom took in Roman and Kaden like they were her own. With Kaden's family wanting nothing to do with him after coming out and Roman's...well...only God knows what country they're traveling to, living life to the fullest, my mom became their mom. She loves it because she always wanted a big family, but due to complications with Glen, they had to stop after him.

I wanted to get her off the phone as quickly as possible. I needed to stop lying to her only to end the conversation with another lie. "Sorry, Mom, but we got a long day ahead of us, so…"

"Okay, sweetheart. You guys have fun. I'll call back sometime during the week."

And hopefully by then I will find them! "Okay, Mom. Love you."

"Love you, too."

Once I hung up, I let out the longest breath ever. It was like I was holding it in for days.

Moments later, I grabbed my stuff and went into Nonoma to tell the sheriff what happened. He said, "Oh, Ashlynn. Why didn't you come to me sooner?"

I honestly didn't have a good answer for him. I replied, "I guess I wasn't thinking straight. I thought they would've returned by now."

He jumped into action. "Alright, darlin' listen, I'm going to file a missing persons' report, but I'm not just going to do it in this county. I'm going to file it in surrounding towns and counties to see if they maybe traveled around."

I was extremely relieved. "Sheriff, I can't thank you enough for doing this for me. It means the world."

He smiled. "Of course, darlin'. Now send me some photos, so I can get this out to the other departments."

I emailed them to him right from my phone.

After walking around town for a little while, showing photos of the boys to people we've gotten to know and to complete strangers, I went back to the cabin empty-handed. I even talked to Charlie to see if he heard from Kaden. He said, "No, I haven't heard from him in maybe a week or two. I thought he lost interest, but this is much worse. I will keep my eye out and spread the word, hon."

I sat in the living room feeling like I got nothing accomplished. Even though I talked to the sheriff and walked around for a good hour, seeing if anybody saw them, I still felt utterly worthless. After a while, I got up and went for a walk in the backyard to clear my mind.

AUGUST 10th

It's been a couple of days and still nothing.

I've walked to the other cabins around Lake Minnetaha, asking whichever neighbors were in town if they saw them. I've been into Nonoma, still asking everyone we've gotten to know if they've seen or heard from them. I've continued going up to complete strangers, showing them their pictures, hoping they might've seen them. Nevertheless, I've gotten the same answer each time. "No. Sorry."

I've visited Sheriff MacReedy practically every day to see if he saw or heard anything from them. His response was continually the same as well. "Sorry, darlin', but I have nothing for you."

Today I said to him, "Damn! I'm so worried about them, Sheriff. I'm starting to fear the worst."

"Now don't think that way, Ms. Ashlynn. I know it's been a week since they left, but please don't worry. They could just be in an area that doesn't have service. Just because this county is 'modernized' doesn't mean all of them are."

"I know, but still. Something about this just doesn't seem right."

We continued talking some more before I remembered, "By the way, have you heard anything from the other towns and counties you reported to?"

He replied, "Sorry, darlin', but I've heard nothing. Now,

not to be rude, but I have some work to do. I'll contact you the second I hear something."

Another day of disappointment and heartbreak!

Will tomorrow be better?

August 11th

Nope, it wasn't.

Today, instead of going into Nonoma, I chose to drive to different nearby towns. Figured instead of going into the same town over and over, maybe I should travel. Maybe I'll find some success.

The first town I drove to I immediately went to the police station. I walked in and was met by Officer Daniels. I told him my story and asked about the missing persons' report. He said, "I don't think we received anything, but I'll double check."

A moment or two later, he came back saying, "I'm sorry, ma'am, but we don't have anything from Amitola Township."

I was appalled. "Are you sure?"

"Yes, ma'am."

I was totally taken aback. "That can't be. I went to him almost a week ago about it and when I saw him yesterday, he made it sound like they were sent out."

The officer shrugged. "I'm sorry, ma'am, but if you want, I'll get one setup for you right now."

"Please, I would really appreciate it."

"Of course. Let me grab some information from you."

I gave him everything he needed. Before I left, he said, "I would check with the other departments to see if Sheriff MacReedy *did* file the reports with them. It seems a little odd that he said he did when we have nothing."

"True. Maybe he thought he did, but actually forgot? Or maybe he hit the wrong button when he sent them out? He is an older guy and sometimes has trouble with his computers and such."

"It's possible, but it's highly irregular for a sheriff, no matter what age, to forget to do their job. And if he's not technologically literate, then he should hire somebody that is."

Damn! He's right! I nodded and agreed. "Thank you so much for your help, Officer Daniels. I'm going to start working my way around and see what happens. Wish me luck."

He smiled. "Good luck, ma'am. I hope you find your brothers soon."

After I left, I immediately went to the next town, heeding the advice of Officer Daniels. To my dismay, the next couple of towns I went to said the same thing, "No report has been filed."

I couldn't believe it. I became irate. I thought, *He couldn't have forgotten every single department within at least a ten-mile radius of Nonoma! I need to talk to him!*

Before I left each station, I made sure to file a report with them to be safe. And while traveling, I did pull over in certain spots to search the forest. I was hoping I would find them or at least signs of them being around, but I found nothing. I left feeling more and more in despair.

On my way back to the cabin, I tried calling Sheriff MacReedy to ask him what was going on, but he didn't answer. The phone at the station kept on ringing and I left a message on his cell. I also texted him asking to call me ASAP as it was about something very important; it was about the boys.

I also passed that damn white building on my way back. I stared at it as if it was calling me, but I kept going. I just wanted to get back to the cabin, shower, rest, and wait for the sheriff to call me back, which he never did.

AUGUST 15th

Days have passed and, you guessed it, still no word from them or from the sheriff. I've called him and texted him multiple times with no answer. My worry and fear have become a full-blown panic. The other day, I almost got into an accident while I was driving because of my lack of sleep and my lack of concentration, so for my safety and the safety of others, I decided to stay in. I literally can't do anything, except for maybe call nearby police stations, stores, hotels, motels, and whatever else I can find. In my eyes, I became useless.

Then this morning, I cracked as I spoke to my mom over the phone. "Mom, I can't hide it anymore! I can't continue lying and I'm so sorry that I have been lying, I just…"

She yelled over me, "Ashlynn, what are you talking about? What's going on?"

I told her everything. She wasn't as pissed as I thought she would be, but she was still mad. "Oh, Ashlynn, why didn't you say something sooner? We could've come up to help."

Through streaming tears, I replied, "I was hoping to have found them by now. I didn't want to burden you guys with this."

That's when my father got on the phone. *Crap, I'm dead!* "Honey, we understand you weren't thinking straight. This is not an easy thing to happen to a young woman. But that doesn't mean we aren't disappointed in you. You're smarter than that!"

"I know, Daddy and I'm sorry."

"It's okay, princess. We're on the next flight out. We'll be up there soon."

And they were. They were at the cabin by the afternoon. They ran in, hugged me, held me, and asked me a thousand questions. We caught up over some lunch before starting the search. I asked if we should go see the sheriff first. My father responded with a vehement, "No! If I see that sheriff, I may punch him in the face!"

My mom gave him a nudge on his arm. "Bob, please. No reason to be so hostile."

"He left our daughter hanging with no answers. I think that's a fair reason to be a little 'hostile.'" He took a deep breathe to calm down. "Plus, at this point, if they're nowhere around here, they must be further out. It's smarter to travel than to stay close."

I wasn't about to argue with him. That's a fair point.

After eating, I called up Mr. Schneider as well to tell him what happened. Before I even asked for more time off, he said, "Ashlynn, take all the time you need. Please be safe and when you find them, I hope they're okay."

After a long day of driving with no results, I went for a walk in the backyard. As I walked around, I smelt something in the air. It smelt like smoke.

It wasn't a strong smell – it seemed to be coming from a distance – but I could smell it. I didn't think anything of it. Figured someone was having a bonfire or had their chimney going. "But it's toward the end of August. It's still pretty nice out," I said to myself. "Unless someone is trying to BBQ and messed up completely."

AUGUST 27th

My mom, my dad, and I continued searching every day for them: going to different towns, walking through the forest…pretty much everything I was doing by myself, but now I had extra eyes.

Today, I finally went back to Nonoma while my parents went to different towns. I immediately went to the sheriff's office to talk to him, but he wasn't there. I went on a hunt for him. I needed to find out why the hell he was dodging me.

I eventually found him by the movie theater talking to some guys. The second I saw him, I did an about-face and stomped over to him. I had a severe bone to pick. The men were dressed in regular clothes, so I thought it wasn't anything important. I tried not to be rude, but at the same time I had *weeks* of pent of frustration to release. Thankfully, they noticed me and immediately left. As they did, the sheriff turned to see me rampaging toward him like a savage animal. Fear flooded his face. "Ms. Ashlynn, are you…"

Before he could utter any other syllables, I shouted, "Who the hell do you think you are?!"

"Excuse me, young lady?!"

"Why haven't you answered any of my calls or texts?! Why have you been avoiding me like I'm the fucking plaque?!"

He raised his voice, something he never did to me, "Watch your language, young lady! I'm the sheriff of this town and I can arrest you for talking to me like that!"

I backed off knowing he was right, and my parents did *not* need that call. We both took in a couple of deep breathes before continuing. I spat out, "I tried calling you and texting you for God knows how long and you've ignored me! No call back, no response, *nothing!* I deserve an explanation!"

His head sank down. He was visibly upset. After letting out a long breathe, he said, "You're probably not going to believe me, darlin', but right after I saw you a couple of weeks back, I dropped my phone and destroyed it. I wasn't able to get a new one until recently and I thought about calling you to check in, but when I didn't see you, I thought you found the boys and went home. I should've gone to the cabin and checked. I'm sorry, sweetheart. I was wrong."

My rage quickly dissipated. Then I remembered, "But what about the missing persons' report? I went to different police stations, and they said you never sent them."

His eyes bugged out. "What do you mean? I sent them."

"Well, according to all of the sheriffs and officers I've talked to, you didn't. They didn't receive anything from you."

I thought for a moment and then something hit him. "Oh, shi…" He looked at me. "Sorry, darlin'."

I smirked. "Sheriff, you know cursing doesn't bother me."

"I know, but it's not proper, especially in front of a young lady. Anyway, I think the reason they didn't receive anything is because as I sent everything out, there was an outage that lasted for a couple of seconds. When the computer came back on, I checked and it showed everything was sent, but I guess it lied to me. Again, I am so sorry, darlin'. Now I understand why you're so angry at me and I would be, too. Can you forgive me?"

My eyes welled up. For weeks I have been so irate with him, but I never knew his side of the story. I never knew what was going on with him. I judged before I was aware of anything. Now it was my turn to beg for forgiveness. "Of course, Sheriff. I'm so sorry for the way I acted. I've been just so worried about the boys."

"Damn, you still haven't found them?"

I shook my head. He came over and gave me a huge bear hug. I tried holding back my tears, but the second he held me, I wept like a baby. "Oh, darlin', I'm so sorry. Please do not despair. I'm sure they're fine and they'll be back soon."

"Boy, Sheriff, I hope you're right. My heart can't handle this anymore."

He continued to hold me and let me cry for a moment or two before letting me go and handing me his handkerchief. I chuckled, "Thank you." As I wiped my tears and regained my composure, I asked, "So who were those guys, if you don't mind me asking?"

"Oh, just some travelers looking for directions."

"Ah." Then I noticed a camera in his hands. "Why do you have your camera, Sheriff?"

"Boy, you like to ask a lot of questions, Ms. Ashlynn," he quipped.

"Yeah, sorry. I guess you can say I'm a little nosy."

He let out that amazing boisterous laugh of his. "No apologies, necessary, darlin'. Well, it's because of that," gesturing toward the movie theater wall.

I looked up to see deep scratch marks in it. I hollered, "Holy shit!" He gave me the side-eye. "Sorry, Sheriff."

He grinned. "It's fine. I had the exact same reaction. It scared the hell out of me."

"And those are some deep scratches, Sheriff. Do you know what it could be from?"

"None. I'm thinking a bear or a bobcat, but I haven't

heard of any animals in the area. And they seem too big to be from an animal."

I stared at the scratches, scrutinizing them, and noticed, "Sheriff, these are definitely not from an animal."

He was stunned. "Are you sure? How do you know?"

"When I was younger, I wanted to work with animals, so I decided to learn more about them. Dogs, cats, birds, wild animals…you name it, I researched it. One thing I remember is how every animal has a different paw print and scratch marks. If these," pointing to the scratches, "were done by like a wildcat, there would be four lines, not five. A bear can leave five marks, but the way these are laid out doesn't lead to a bear either."

"So what do you think made them?"

I looked at him. "A human."

We stared at each other in disbelief. *I* couldn't even believe I said that. He exclaimed, "A human?!"

"I know but look." I put my hand against the wall and mimicked the act. Except for the fact that the mark was huge, it matched.

Sheriff MacReedy became as white as a ghost. He stuttered, "That's a great observation, Ash. I have to go now and write a report. See ya later," and abruptly left.

"Oh, okay…see ya," I replied watching him move so quickly, I thought smoke was coming out of his shoes. Then I panned back to the marks. I continued studying them for a little while longer before leaving.

SEPTEMBER 24th

I can't believe it's been over a month with nothing from Roman, Kaden, or Glen; no one hearing anything, no one seeing anything, and complete silence from them. I'm still not sleeping well because I'm thinking at one point they'll either call or return. I've been talking to the sheriff, as well, and still nothing on his end.

I'm so disheartened. I'm starting to think they're dead. My parents are trying to stay positive, but I could tell they are just as heartbroken. To make matters worse, my mom got a call this afternoon that her mom – my grandmother – fell and broke her hip. She cried, "Things just can't get any worse right now." I held her while my dad rubbed her back. We did all we could to comfort her. "What do I do? I'm stuck in between a rock and a hard place right now. I should stay and look for my boys, but I need to go take care of my mom."

I suggested, "Why don't you and Dad go home. I'll stay until October, which is in a week. If still nothing, it'll mark two months that they're gone. I'll come home and let the sheriff and other cops in the area take care of it."

"We're not leaving you here alone," my dad retorted.

"I was alone for some time, Dad, and I was fine."

"Yeah, that was before we knew the truth, which don't think I forgot about, young lady." I rolled my eyes. "No, we're not leaving you unless someone is here with you."

I thought for a moment and remembered. "Wait, I think

Mr. Scarlo is up here for the fall season. Why don't we ask him?"

My parents looked at each other and agreed, "That's not a bad idea."

He's an old family friend who lives across the lake from us. He's originally from San Francisco and is a little out there, but he's a sweetheart. He's in his forties, but he always acts like he's my age. My dad called him up and explained the situation. Within minutes he was over.

We spent the rest of the night catching up, telling him what happened with the boys, and talking about what's going on in life. Even though there were moments of sadness, they were trumped by the moments of happiness. It felt so good to hear laughter in the cabin again.

SEPTEMBER 25th

This morning, my parents left. Mr. Scarlo was over to see them off. My dad said to him, "Ned, we cannot thank you enough for helping us out and watching Ashlynn."

"Please, Bob. Your family has always been like mine. I just hope Nancy's mom gets well soon. And don't worry, we'll find Glen and the others."

My dad nodded. He gave me a hug and said, "Don't you do anything stupid, princess."

"Now where's the fun in that." We both laughed. "Don't worry, Daddy. I'll be fine," I said holding him tight.

Both of my parents gave me hugs and kisses before they departed.

Mr. Scarlo stayed over after they left and made me some breakfast. As we ate, he asked, "So what can I do today to help find the boys?"

I answered, "That's really sweet of you, Mr. Scarlo, but I think this week I'm going to stay back at the cabin and rest. I feel like I got run over by an 18-wheeler."

"I completely understand, sweetie, but that didn't answer my question."

I grinned. "You're right. I'm sorry. I can't even think straight," I said as I rubbed my forehead.

"It's okay, hon," he gently rubbed my back. "How about this? I'll contact some of my friends in the area and see if they know anything. Maybe they can help us out."

I became excited. "That sounds great! Thanks, Mr. Scarlo."

"Of course. Now go rest. I'll take care of cleaning up."

And that's exactly what I did. I sat on the couch in the family room and watched some TV. However, as I sat there, listening to Mr. Scarlo making his calls, I felt even worse. I felt like I needed to do something. *But what else can I do? I've been to every town within a twenty mile or so radius of this lake and I'm sure my parents went further. I've talked to Sheriff MacReedy and the departments in the other towns. I've pretty much killed myself to find them, and I have no clue if they're even alive.*

While these thoughts flooded my mind, I cried hysterically. Mr. Scarlo saw and came over to comfort me. "Aw, Ashlynn, what's wrong, hon?"

I sobbed, "It's been two months. I've searched everywhere for them, and I can't find them. They're most likely dead."

"No, Ashlynn, don't think like that." He tried his hardest to comfort me, but it wasn't working. Then he asked, "Why did you stay then if this is how you feel?"

It took me a minute to answer. I had to think about it. *Why did I stay?* Then I remembered. "Because as they left, Kaden said, 'We'll be watching over you.' I don't think they went anywhere far if that was the case, right?"

"I think you're exactly right." I figured he was just saying that to make feel better, which kind of helped. "Here, let me make you a cup of my tea. A cup of Mr. Scarlo's tea will always bring you relief."

I laughed. He wasn't kidding though. Whenever he makes tea, you always feel ten times better. I think he puts something in it to help you feel uber relaxed, but I've never watched him make it, so I can't say for sure.

After drinking Mr. Scarlo's amazing tea and relaxing for some time, I decided to go for a walk in the backyard. I wandered through the woods for a good hour and got pretty far from the cabin. I felt at home in the woods. I felt composed. I actually talked out loud while walking. "They can't be dead. My boys are so strong. They can fight anything, whether it's a cold or a bear. They're nearby. I know they are. One day I'm going to look up and they'll be right in front of my face."

As I continued walking, I began to hear twigs snapping and leaves crunching under a heavy foot. I looked around to find nothing. No animal. No person. I said, "Okay, now I'm convinced Mr. Scarlo puts something in his tea. He needs to share that shit. It's amazing!"

Then I looked down and saw a huge footprint in the ground. It looked human, but it was massive and somewhat deformed. My heart leapt into my throat. I couldn't believe what I was seeing. I thought, *Is Bigfoot in my backyard?*

The snapping of twigs and the crunching of leaves persisted, but it was all around me. I scanned around and still found nothing. "Alright, Mr. Scarlo doesn't have to share with me. This is a little much."

I panicked and quickly went back to the cabin. As I walked in, Mr. Scarlo was sitting on the couch. He looked up and saw I was a little skittish. "You okay, love?"

I looked at him. "I think I'm seriously losing my mind."

He chuckled. "Why? What makes you say that?"

Still trying to catch my breath, I replied, "Because I swear to God, I just found a Bigfoot footprint not too far from the cabin."

He looked away. "Oh, well, that's interesting."

I was confused. "Why?"

"Because we haven't had a Bigfoot sighting since the eighties," he panned back to me with a smirk on his face.

I tittered as I rubbed my face and hair trying to quiet my mind. He got up and walked over to me, gently rubbed my shoulders, and said, "Relax, sweetie. It was probably a bear print that you mistook for something else. There might be an animal control law here, but we still get them every so often." *I may not be all there, but I know what I saw!* He wrapped his arm around my shoulders and gently led me to the couch. "Why don't you sit down, and I'll make you some tea."

My eyes widened. "Actually, I think I'm good, Mr. Scarlo. Having one of *your* teas a day is more than I can handle."

We stopped. "Honey, I wasn't talking about *my* tea. Everyone can handle my tea only once a day." We laughed.

Once the morning turned into night, Mr. Scarlo left to take care of his little chihuahua, Mr. Bojangles. I told him he could bring him over. "You know I love dogs."

He replied, "I know, sweetie, but he has his special spots that he likes to sleep and go potty, so I'm not going to mess that up for him."

"Okay, then I'll see you tomorrow?"

"Bright and early."

"Please, not too early, Mr. Scarlo. I do want to try and get some sleep."

"Understandable. How about around ten or eleven then."

"Perfect. Thank you, Mr. Scarlo."

"You're very welcome, Ashlynn. Good night."

Soon after he left, I went back to the couch to continue watching TV where I eventually fell asleep.

SEPTEMBER 26th

When I woke up this morning, I had a massive kink in my neck. "Well, I'm never sleeping on the couch again, if you even call that sleeping." I was constantly tossing and turning, having some very weird dreams, or least I hope they were dreams. I have no clue if I was awake or not, but I kept on seeing these bright red eyes by the windows.

Around 10:30, Mr. Scarlo showed up. He came in hollering, "Wakey, wakey!"

I replied, somewhat irritated, "I'm awake, Mr. Scarlo."

"Good because I'm about to make some breakfast."

Then he saw me hunched over with my head tilted to one side. "Don't even tell me you slept on that couch the entire night."

My eyes shifted. "Okay, I won't."

He sighed. "Here, let me help you out."

He came over and started rubbing my neck, shoulders, and upper back. Little by little, I was able to move my neck again. "Oh, wow. This feels amazing, Mr. Scarlo. Since when are you a massage therapist?"

"Since I decided to take some classes to meet this guy only to find out he had a boyfriend."

"That bastard!"

He laughed. "I know, right?! But I learned a great skill that led me to this other guy."

"Wait, does that mean?"

"Yuppers!"

"Aw, yea! I'm so happy for you, Mr. Scarlo!"

"Thanks, sweetie."

"So, where is he? I want to meet him."

"He'll be down later in October. Right now, he's traveling for work."

As he continued to massage me, he told me more about his new boyfriend. After about a half hour or so, I was able to move my neck again. "Ah, that's so much better. Thank you."

"You're welcome. Now, what lesson did we learn?"

"Not to sleep on the couch," I grumbled like a teenager.

Later in the day, I went for another walk in the woods. I figured what happened yesterday was a "reaction" from Mr. Scarlo's tea, which I learned to only drink at night. However, as I walked around, I found one of Kaden's shirts lying on a branch; like it was purposefully put there. I ran to it and grabbed it. "Kaden," I said softly to the shirt, as if it would answer me. I held it against my chest. I teared up. I then held it up to see it had been torn to shreds. I was horrified. "Oh, god, Kaden! What the hell happened?"

That's when I heard heavy footsteps running away, but they were a distance ahead of me. I looked up, excitedly yelled, "Kaden," and ran toward them. I continued yelling, "Kaden! Wait!" Then I heard them stop. I also stopped and looked around. "Kaden?" I saw nothing, but I heard something heavily breathing. It almost sounded like when a bulldog or a pug is breathing heavily. Kind of a wheezing sound. "Kaden! It's Ashlynn!"

I walked around trying to follow the sound of the breathing, but it seemed like it was coming from every direction. I couldn't pinpoint it. I looked for tracks or any other signs of Roman, Kaden, or Glen being nearby. As per usual, I found nothing. My heart sank further and further. I fell to the ground, gripping Kaden's shirt, and cried. I wailed,

"Please don't leave me again, Kaden!"

From behind me I heard Mr. Scarlo calling my name. I guess he heard me screaming and came looking for me. When he found me, he ran over to me, "Honey, what happened?" He fell beside me and held me. He saw the shirt in my hand. He grabbed it, "What's this?"

Through tears, I responded, "Kaden's shirt."

"Aw, sweetie," he said, sympathetically. He tried pulling me up. "Come on, let's get back to the cabin," but I fought him.

I screamed, "No, I'm not leaving!"

He continued pulling me away and I continued fighting. He was getting angry, but I could also hear fear in his voice. "Ashlynn, we need to leave now!"

"You go back to the cabin! I'm not leaving un…"

"Ashlynn Angela Amuso, you are coming back to the cabin with me right now or else!"

I was stunned. Mr. Scarlo never yells. I've never seen him get so upset. Through streaming tears, I said, "I'm sorry, Mr. Scarlo. I…"

He relaxed a bit. "It's okay, sweetie. Let's just get back to the cabin. I'll make you a cup of tea. I think we'll both need it tonight."

As he helped me back, I noticed he kept on looking around, but I didn't even bother to ask why. I was still in so much shock from finding Kaden's shirt.

After drinking some tea, the rest of the night became a blur.

SEPTEMBER 27th

After sleeping pretty well, thanks to Mr. Scarlo's tea, I woke up and called my parents to tell them what I found. One of the plethora of questions they asked was, "How do you know it was deliberately placed there? It could've been there this entire time."

I retorted, "Because I went past the same area the other day, and nothing was there."

They had no response.

Not too long after I got off the phone with them, Mr. Scarlo walked in. "Good morning."

"Good morning, Mr. Scarlo."

"How are we doing today? Better?"

"Yeah, a little."

He came over and sat next to me at the dining room table. "Good, I'm glad to hear."

"Listen, Mr. Scarlo. I just want to apologize for yesterday."

He held up his hand. "No need to apologize, sweetie. If anything, I should apologize to you for dragging you away. I just got really creeped out."

"Really? By what?"

"Well, I thought I saw something darting around in the forest, so I wanted to get us back to the safety of the cabin as quickly as possible."

"Oh, interesting." Then I asked, "Do you remember

what I did with Kaden's shirt? I've been looking for it, but I can't find it."

"Yeah, I think I grabbed it from you and left it out there," pointing to the backyard.

My heart sank. "Oh, no. I wanted to hold onto it just in case I never found them."

Mr. Scarlo gasped and covered his mouth. "Aw, honey, I'm so sorry." He felt horrible. He removed his hands from his mouth and said, "I'll run out there later and get it for you."

"No, you don't have to do that Mr. Scarlo; especially…"

He stopped me. "I want too. My way of begging for your forgiveness." I grinned. He continued, "So I was thinking maybe you should go for a drive today. See some different scenery. Maybe that'll clear your head a bit."

I nodded. "That's not a bad idea." *I have calmed down enough to drive again!*

He joked, "Hopefully nothing happens to make you question your sanity."

"Yeah, hopefully."

While driving I found the first place Roman, Kaden, Glen, and I stopped at on our first ride. I parked, got out, and stood exactly where we did, taking in the beauty of the world. I fell to my knees and cried hysterically, "I'm so sorry. I should've fought harder."

I stayed for a little while longer before continuing my drive. At one point, I came to the road that led to the white building. I was hesitant to take it, but I did. Every time I have driven past that damn building, I have felt drawn to it. I never stopped to look at it…until today. I parked my car, got out, and just glared at it. However, while doing so, I noticed something wasn't right. I saw a little bit of smoke coming from it. My eyes widened. "Oh my gosh!"

I ran up to see if anybody needed help. My mom was a paramedic and I got to watch her help people in need, so I guess I inherited that from her. I went up to the fence and yelled, "Hello!"

There wasn't an answer. I scanned around to find no one. Ahead of me was a heavy-looking metal door with an "Exit" sign above it. It was open with some lingering smoke coming out of it. I again yelled, "Hello," with no answer. I wanted to make sure no one was harmed, but I also wanted to see what the hell happened in there. With a lot of hesitation, I forced myself to climb over the chain-link fence to take a closer look.

This is a bad idea, Ash! A very bad idea!

Walking up to it I already felt an uneasiness. As I went toward the door, I once again yelled, "Hello?"

Still no answer. I slowly looked in. It looked like some sort of lab with a bunch of different equipment set up all over. I walked in and asked, "Is anyone here?"

I roamed around trying to figure out what went on in it, but everything was strewn about and broken. Ahead of me was another door, wide open with the lights flickering on and off. As I stepped toward it, there was a loud bang, like something hit against a metal locker. I jumped. "Is someone there?"

Silence.

"I'm here to help! Let me know if you're hurt!"

Still silence.

My mind was screaming, *You need to get the fuck out of here, Ash!* But something was luring me toward that room. I went to it and looked in. There were metal cages big enough to hold a person in it. They were ripped apart. The metal bars were bent outward as if whatever was in them let themselves out. Tables were flipped over, and papers were all over the place. It was like a war zone.

I walked over to the cages to study them because, again, I'm so goddamn nosy. I thought, *Whomever bent these bars must have Herculean strength! There's no way a normal human could've bent them like this unless they were extremely hot!*

As I continued peering around, I noticed on one of the walls there was a corkboard with photos on it. I looked at them. They were "Before" and "After" photos of young men who went from looking normal to looking different. Almost like Captain America: going from being this scrawny guy to a contestant for Mr. Olympia. They were the ones that "Passed".

Below them were the ones that "Failed", but with only "Before" pictures. There were no "After". *I guess they must've died, but from what?*

Going through the photos, I came across one where the guy looked familiar. It was partially burnt, so I couldn't see his whole face. I went to look closer when I heard a door slam, hard, behind me. I screamed and turned to find another door, closed. With my heart racing and my voice shaking, I asked, "Is someone there?"

The answer was something scratching against the metal door and growling. I yelled, "Fuck this" and ran out the door. I raced to my car, got in, and sped away. I wasn't about to find out what was behind that door.

****

As I arrived back at the cabin, I walked in to Mr. Scarlo

running to me, screaming, "We need to get the heck out of here!"

I sprung out of my skin. "What the hell are you talking about?"

He came over to me and put his hands on my shoulders. "We need to leave this cabin right now, Ashlynn! When I went to go retrieve the shirt for you, I saw this thing with bright red eyes! I can't explain it, but it wasn't an animal nor was it a person!"

While he talked, I thought back to the night I dreamt of seeing red eyes out the living room window. *Maybe it wasn't a dream!*

"Let's go to my cabin now!" he said, huffing and puffing.

Even though I believed him after what I experienced at the white building, I still teased, "Mr. Scarlo, did you have some of your tea?"

"Ashlynn, I'm not joking. I know what I saw. Let's leave and go to my cabin now!" he demanded.

Inside, my whole body was screaming, "He's right! Something is going on here! We should leave!" But I stubbornly stood my ground. "With all due respect, Mr. Scarlo, how do you know it's not by your cabin? And why didn't you call the sheriff?"

"I did and he didn't believe me."

"Really? Why didn't he believe you?"

"His exact words were, 'Monsters don't exist, Ned. Stop drinking your tea or taking whatever would make me arrest you.' Can you believe that?"

I was disgusted. "Wait, what?!"

He threw his hands in the air. "Exactly! Between being

hurt, being scared, and being angry, I'm just a ball of flipping nerves."

"Hold on," I unzipped my purse, "let me try calling him and talking to him. He'll believe me."

I grabbed my phone to only realize it died. "God dammit. Piece of shit died on me."

"Ashlynn, what did I say about your cursing?" he shouted with his hands on his hips.

"I've gotten better."

He rolled his eyes.

"Let me go charge it, so I can call him later."

I started walking toward my room when Mr. Scarlo grabbed my arm. "Honey, just grab your charger, so we can go. I don't want to stay here any longer." The look I gave must've scared him because he let go of my arm and said, "Please."

Living in New York, a girl must keep her guard up and him grabbing me, triggered me. However, I snapped back to reality and apologized profusely. "I'm so sorry, Mr. Scarlo. I didn't mean to scare you."

He put his hands up. "Again, no apologies necessary, hon. I completely understand, but please grab your charger and some stuff to stay overnight. With it getting darker out," we both looked out the windows to see the sun setting, "I don't want to be here if that thing is still out there."

I sighed. "Look, Mr. Scarlo. I'm tired and the way I feel, I don't think even Bigfoot would mess with me. I just want to try and get some sleep in my own bed."

He nodded. I could tell he hated the idea of leaving me here alone, but also knew this was a losing battle. He said, "I can respect that, but please call me the second you wake up that way I know you're okay."

"Of course, Mr. Scarlo. I will."

We hugged each other and he left. After he did, I plopped down on the couch and asked myself, "What the fuck is going on around here?!"

SEPTEMBER 28th

Not too long after waking up, I did as I was asked; I called Mr. Scarlo. He was still shaken up. He told me he was leaving, going back to San Francisco until it was safe again. He said he had to think about himself and Mr. Bojangles. He also didn't want his boyfriend, David, to come here and have something happen to him. I replied, "I completely understand," and we pretty much left it at that.

After talking to him, I did a couple of chores around the cabin before sitting in the living room to look out the window and relax. I joked, "I'm in the cabin! Nothing can go wrong, right?"

While staring out into the world, I saw something out of the ordinary. It was standing next to a tree, almost blending in with it until I saw it was breathing. I continued watching it, focusing in on it. That's when I saw these piercing red eyes staring back at me. I closed my eyes tightly and shook my head, hoping when I opened them it would be gone. "Nothing's there, Ash. You're just seeing things," I said, trying to convince myself.

I slowly opened them, and the thing was closer. I got so scared that I stood up quickly, knocking over the chair I was sitting on, and tripping over the damn thing. I fell to the floor, hard, landing on my elbow. When I did, I saw stars. It took me a bit to get up, but when I did, whatever I saw was gone. I was in tears rubbing my elbow, I was in so much pain. "Shit! That was really fucking graceful, Ash!"

I eventually got up and went to the window. I glared out, trying to find something to explain what I saw. *What the hell was that? Are my eyes playing tricks on me? Am I going insane? Is that what Mr. Scarlo saw?*

So many questions ran through my head, and I didn't know what to do next. *Should I call the sheriff? He didn't believe Mr. Scarlo when he called him, which I still need to talk to him about, but will he believe me? He should! He knows I don't lie! Maybe I should call home? Hear a comforting voice to…*

Then a sharp pain reverberated throughout my elbow. I looked down at it; it was swollen. "But first, I should probably put some ice on this," I said, wincing in pain.

Upon grabbing the ice, I decided to call home. I wanted to hear my mom's voice.

"Hello?" my mom answered, sounding exhausted.

"Hi, Mom."

"Oh, hi, Ashlynn! How's my little girl doing?"

"I'm doing okay. What about you? You sound tired."

"Yeah, well between taking care of Nana and worrying about the boys, I haven't gotten much sleep."

"I hear ya on that. How's she doing?"

"Getting better, little by little. So what's going on on your end? Find anything else that could lead to the boys."

"No, but…" I hesitated, pondering if I should tell her. "I, uh…"

"What sweetie?" she asked, concerned.

"I saw something strange in the woods, which is why I'm calling you. I needed to hear your voice and 'chillax.'"

She wasn't entirely amused. "Very funny, Ashlynn." We both chuckled. "Now what did you see?"

"That's the thing, I don't know. I mean, I guess the best way I can describe it is…it looked like a monster."

She stuttered, "I'm sorry, what?"

I took in a deep breath and walked over to the window. "What I saw out in the woods looked like a monster. It was massive with these bright red eyes."

She was at a loss for words. "Are you sure you saw what you saw?"

"No, because I tripped over the rocking chair in the living room and when I got up nothing was there."

She gasped. "Oh my goodness, sweetie. Are you okay?"

"Eh. My elbow's banged up, but otherwise I'm okay."

She became upset. "Oh gosh, Ashlynn. If anything happens to *you* now…"

"Mom, I'm fine," I practically yelled at her.

She stopped, taking in a couple of breaths. "I'm sorry, Ash. I…just…"

It sounded like she was crying or was about to. I replied tenderly, "I know, Mom. I know."

I gave her a minute to regain her composure while I continued scanning the backyard to see if I could find anything strange or out of the ordinary, but everything seemed normal. She continued, "Okay, so back to what you saw. You know, it could have been a figment of your imagination. You do love those damn horror movies, why I'll never understand." I rolled my eyes. *Says the one who goes for a good true crime documentary!* "Maybe you daydreamed it," she said while also questioning.

"It's possible."

"Is Ned with you? Did you have some of his tea?"

I laughed. "No, but he actually saw something as well by

the cabin and left the area this morning."

She was shocked. "Really? He didn't call to tell me."

"He was in a rush to leave, he got so scared. I guess he didn't even think of it."

"Oh. Maybe you should come home too, then."

"No, Mom, I want to stay. If I didn't find anything leading to the boys, that would be one thing, but finding Kaden's shirt yesterday means they're nearby. I feel it. I don't want to leave now when I'm so close."

She groaned. "Ugh, you're so stubborn! Just like your father!"

We talked for a little bit longer before she said, "I'm sorry, sweetie, but I have to go check on Nana."

"Okay, Mom. I love you and please send her my love."

"I will. I love you, too, sweetheart."

Once I hung up with her, I took in another deep breath, continued staring out the window, and thought about what she said. *Maybe she's right! Maybe I did imagine it!*

Then I felt another sharp pain in my elbow. I looked at it. It looked like the swelling went down, but now it was starting to bruise.

"Then again, maybe I didn't."

****

I looked online to see if there was a doctor nearby still open to call about my elbow. Thankfully, there was. I called and told him what happened. He said, "I would really like you to come in, so I can take an X-ray; make sure nothing is broken."

"But Dr. Park, I'm about a half hour away from you."

"It's okay. I'll stay open and wait for you. It's not a problem."

I drove as fast as I could. When I got there, he took the X-ray, which showed nothing was broken. As he was putting my arm in a sling, he stated, "It looks like it's just bruised, Ashlynn, which is good. However, if the pain persists or you notice you can't move it, then I'll give you a script to get an MRI at the hospital. I can only do so much in my little office." We both laughed. "For now, don't do too much with this arm…" *Great! I'm a righty! This is going to be fun!* "…and please don't fall on it again. Otherwise, you'll be fine."

"Sounds good. Thanks, Dr. Park."

"My pleasure. So, what happened that made you fall on your elbow in the first place?" he inquired, stepping away and leaning on a counter.

"I, uh, thought I saw something outside my living room, and it scared me so much that I tripped over my rocking chair."

"Oh boy! What did you see? A bear?"

I thought about what to say. *Do I tell him the truth? Let him think I'm crazy!* I answered, "I think so. I'm not a hundred percent sure though. It all kind of happened in the blink of an eye." *Not 100% a lie, but not 100% the truth either!*

"I see. Well, whatever it was it must've been a sight, huh? I mean the animal control law is great, but it's nice to see some wild animals from time to time. Remind us we're not the only ones on this planet, you know."

I nodded. "Very true, doc."

He went on to explain to me how to use the sling (couple of hours on, couple of hours off type of deal) that way my arm didn't get too stiff and told me to take some aspirin for the pain. But he reminded me if the pain persisted for a couple of days to come back.

As the sun began to set, I pulled into the driveway and saw a note on the door. I looked at it. The writing seemed childish, but it said, "Ashlynn, we hope you're okay. We're fine. Please go home. Love you."

My heart raced. I ran around the cabin into the woods screaming their names. I didn't run too far in, but at one point I stopped, continuing to scream their names. Once again, I saw and heard nothing. I fell to my knees crying. I yelled out, "I'm not leaving you! Please come back!"

After sobbing for some time, I heard heavy footsteps coming toward me. I looked up to see the same piercing red eyes from earlier staring at me from behind a tree. I screamed and scrambled to get up and run. I flew into the cabin and locked all of the doors and windows. I went to draw the blinds to be reminded that my mom made sure we didn't have blinds or curtains in the cabin. "I'm not covering up this view," was her reason.

"God damnit, Mom!" I ran to my purse and grabbed my phone. "Fuck this, I'm calling the sheriff!"

I called his cell with no answer. "Oh, don't even tell me you broke it again." I then tried his office. After a couple of rings, he answered, "Sheriff's office."

I frantically replied, "Sheriff, it's Ashlynn!"

"Ms. Ashlynn. You okay, darlin'?"

"No, Sheriff, I'm not okay. There's something here at the cabin."

"What, darlin'?" he asked, concerned.

"Honestly, I have no other way to describe it other than a monster. It blends in with the trees, but it's eyes are red like fire, and it has sharp teeth and…"

He cut me short. "Okay, darlin', okay. Let's first take a

couple of deep breaths and calm down."

I did. He continued, "Now, your neighbor, Mr. Scarlo called yesterday with the same story. Are you sure you saw what you saw?"

"Yes, Sheriff! You know me! I wouldn't make this shit up!"

"Ms. Ashlynn, the cursing!"

"Oh, never mind about my cursing right now, Sheriff! I'm scared out of my god damn mind!"

He let out a long breathe. "Did you have any of your neighbor's tea?"

I was shocked. "You don't believe me."

"Now, Ms. Ashlynn, I didn't say…"

"No, it's fine, Sheriff. Don't believe me. But when you find my body torn to shreds, please explain to my parents why my blood is on your fucking hands," and then I hung up.

"Fuck!" I sobbed, "What do I do now?"

I was half-tempted to pack up and leave, but as the light slipped into darkness, I was terrified to go outside by myself. I was also hoping that the sheriff would come and arrest me for what I said, but as the minutes ticked by, no sirens were heard, and no cars came. I thought, *Jesus, I'm living in my own horror movie! Seriously, who do I call next? My mother thinks it's a figment of my imagination and the sheriff thinks I'm on a drug bender! Who the hell else can I turn to?*

That's when it hit me. I literally palmed my forehead with my good hand as I said, "Jack, you moron!"

Jack's someone I've literally known my whole life. He's a cryptozoologist: someone who studies obscure creatures like Bigfoot and the Loch Ness monster. If anyone would believe me, it would be him. The line on the other end only rang once. "Hey, beautiful," he answered, excitedly.

Trying to sound calm, I said, "Hey, Jack! What's going on?"

"Nothing much. You? How's the vacation?"

"It's, uh…"

He could hear in my voice something wasn't right. "Ash, what's wrong?" he asked, worried.

"I need your help," my voice trembled. "There's something here that's not human, Jack. I'm scared out of my mind, and no one is believing me."

"It's okay, Ash. I believe you," he said with no hesitation.

I smirked, but I was still freaking out. "Thank you, Jack, but I don't know what to do. I'm afraid to leave. Do you think you can come out to Washington?"

"Yeah, of course. Wait…you're still at the cabin?"

"Yeah, it's a long story."

"Okay, well, would it be okay if my crew came along?"

"Your crew?"

"Yeah, for the show."

"Oh, shit! I completely forgot your working on your show! I'm so sorry, Jack!"

He chuckled. "It's fine, hon, no worries. Is it okay though?"

"Well, I was thinking you could just come up and get me, but…"

"Oh, yeah, of course, I was just…"

"No, no, please bring your crew. Whatever is here might make for a great episode."

He laughed. "Great. Give me one second."

I couldn't believe I forgot he was greenlit for a TV show about going around the world searching for strange beings and phenomena. I was so mad at myself. As I continued yelling at myself – in my head – for being such a dumbass, I heard him mumbling to someone about looking up plane tickets to Seattle and rental cars. While he did, I kept on looking out the window to see if it was back. At one point, my state of paranoia broke when I heard Jack say, "That can wait. She's way more important." I felt my little smirk turn into a broad smile.

A moment later, he came back on the line, "Sorry, Ash, we're just looking up plane tickets. So what's going on? I texted you toward the end of August to check and see if you guys were still coming, but I didn't hear anything back. I figured you went back home."

Damnit! Another thing I forgot about! "I know and I'm so sorry I never answered you, Jack. Things have been really crazy here." I went on to tell him what's been going on.

With sympathy, he replied, "Aw, Ashlynn, I'm so sorry to hear, hon. Why didn't you call me earlier?"

"Well, for one, I haven't been thinking straight."

"Understandable."

"And two, I didn't want to bother you."

"Please, hon. I would've dropped everything to have been there for you. You are never bothering me."

My heart fluttered. "Thanks, Jack. That means a lot."

It sounded like he was about to say something when he was interrupted by someone telling him they found a flight leaving at nine in the morning from Sacramento to Seattle.

"Awesome. What about a rental?"

"Working on that right now."

I interjected, "You know, I can always come and pick you guys up. Save you some money."

"Nah, that's okay, hon. That's what the budget is for."

I laughed. He continued, "So it looks like we got a flight leaving for nine tomorrow morning. How far is the cabin from Seattle's airport again?"

"About an hour and a half."

"Okay, so figure by the time we land, grab our stuff, and get the rental, we should be at your place around one."

I felt so relieved. "That sounds great."

"Please make sure all the windows and doors are locked tonight and try to stay calm. I'll see you tomorrow."

"Awesome. Thank you so much, Jack, for doing this. And I'm sorry if I'm putting you guys out or stopping you from..."

He stopped me, "It's not a problem, hon. You know I'd do anything for you at any time," somehow my smile grew bigger, "so don't you apologize for anything. I'll call you as we leave the airport, okay?"

"Alright, sounds good. Good night, Jack."

"Night, hon."

I felt so much better after I got off the phone with him. I felt comforted, like a weight was lifted off my shoulders. *Finally, someone who believes me and is willing to help me!*

****

Before I went to shower, I double-checked to make sure all the doors and windows were locked. I continued looking out the windows to find nothing was there. I said to myself, "Alright, Ash, just go take a shower and get some sleep."

As I walked back toward my room and bathroom, I thought, *Man, Mr. Scarlo's tea would be really helpful right about now!*

While I was showering, I thought I heard something over the water running and my music playing, but I ignored it. It wasn't until I turned the water off that I realized I *was* hearing something. I turned off my music to listen; it sounded like a scratching noise. I wrapped my towel as tight as I could around my body, opened the bathroom door, and went to my room. That's where the scratches were the loudest. I also heard the same heavy breathing I heard the other day and growling. My eyes blazed with fear. I thought, *Oh my gosh! That thing is right outside my room!*

I froze in place, barely breathing, afraid it might hear me.

Seconds later, it stopped grating at the cabin, let out this horrifying roar, and ran off. I crept into my room trying not to make a sound. I didn't know if it was still nearby. I grabbed my phone from its charger, ran back into the bathroom, slammed the door, and locked it. I immediately called Jack. This time, though, the phone kept on ringing. *Shit, he's probably asleep!*

Suddenly, "Hey, Ash," he answered breathing somewhat heavily. "Is everything okay?"

"It was outside my room, Jack."

"What?!"

"I heard it right outside my bedroom."

"Where are you? Are you okay?"

"Yeah, I locked myself in the bathroom."

"Okay good," he was so relieved to hear. "What sound was it making?"

"It was breathing and growling, but it was also scratching at the cabin, like it was digging a hole into it."

"And did it?"

"No, thankfully it didn't. It stopped, roared like a dinosaur, and ran away. Or at least I think it did."

"Do you hear any noises right now?"

"No, but…" I stopped talking to listen for anything out of the ordinary. That's when I heard faint cries and screams. I whispered, "Hold on," into the phone. I unlocked the bathroom door and opened it a little. As I did, I heard the sounds a little clearer. I asked, "Do you hear that, Jack?"

"No," he replied. "What is it?"

"It sounds like cries and screams from an animal."

I fully opened the door and slowly went into my room. Those cries and screams got louder and clearer. I, then, said, "Hold on, let me put you on speaker." I figured maybe me holding the phone to my ear was muffling the noise. "Can you hear it now?"

"A little."

We both stayed silent for a moment listening, wondering. "What the hell is that?" he asked.

I shook my head as if he could see me. Then there was another roar, similar to what I heard earlier, but it wasn't just from one creature. It sounded like there were at least two or three of them that roared. I jumped, almost dropping my phone. "Did you hear that?"

"Loud and clear! Holy shit! Seriously, what the hell is that?"

Soon after those roars, all the sounds stopped. "Oh god, do you hear that?"

"No, I hear nothing."

"Exactly." I ran back into the bathroom. "Jack, I don't know if I can stay here tonight," I shouted as tears welled up in my eyes.

He snapped, "No, don't you dare go outside. That thing could be anywhere."

I slowly sat down on the toilet bowl lid, shocked that Jack actually kind of yelled at me. He immediately apologized. "I didn't mean to yell, hon. I just wish I could be there to protect you."

With a tear or two running down my cheeks, I beamed. "Me too."

"But it's going to be okay. We'll be there tomorrow, and you won't have to worry anymore."

We continued to talk for a little while longer until I felt a little better. Once I got off the phone with him, I finished getting dressed. I tiptoed into my room and onto my bed, not wanting to make a sound. I didn't even want to breathe fearing that thing could hear me and burst through the wall to get me. As I tried to get some sleep, every little sound I heard made me wonder, *Oh god, is it back?*

I tried to think of the safest place for me to sleep in because my bedroom didn't feel safe at the moment. *I guess I'm heading back to the bathroom*, I thought because its walls don't lead to the outside and if I made any noise in it, no one would hear. I grabbed my phone, my charger, my pillow, and a fleece blanket. I slunk back to the bathroom, turned on the light, closed the door, and locked it. Then I looked down at the tile floor. "Shit, that ain't going to be comfortable. I have to go grab some more blankets."

We kept them in the same room Kaden slept in. I haven't been in that room since the day they left. When I opened the door and turned on the light, my eyes widened, and my heart leapt into my throat. Kaden's shirt was perfectly sprawled out on his bed. I looked around, questioning, "How? How is this here?"

I sat on his bed and wept. "Oh, Kaden. What happened to you? Where are you? I want you home."

Absentmindedly, I laid on his bed and continued to cry into his shirt until I eventually fell asleep.

SEPTEMBER 29th

I woke up in the middle of the night realizing where I was. I instantly shot up, looked around, and listened for any strange noises. When I heard nothing, I crawled off the bed, and went back to the bathroom with Kaden's shirt still in my hand. I accepted my fate of lying on the cold tile floor and tried falling back to sleep. I had a little help from the videos I watched on my phone as I cradled Kaden's shirt in my arms.

****

Around 10:30, my phone went off waking me up. It was Jack. He told me they had just landed and were about to grab their gear and the rental car. I slowly got up to get ready. Between my back and my elbow, I was in pain. *A massage from Mr. Scarlo would be extremely helpful right about now!*

Before I started getting ready, I folded up Kaden's shirt and put it into one of my drawers. I said, "Soon, I'm going to give this back to you, my friend. I promise."

It was late in the afternoon when Jack and his crew pulled up. As they got out of the car and grabbed their stuff, I opened the door and swiftly walked up to them. "Jack!"

He looked up. "Ash!" and then saw my arm in the sling. "Oh gosh, babe," he ran over to me. "Is that," pointing to my elbow, "what you were talking about yesterday?"

"Yup."

He grimaced in pain. "Nothing is broken, though, right?"

His crew began to surround us. I replied, grabbing onto the sling, "Yeah, nothing's broken. Just bruised and sore as hell."

He gave me a sad face. "Can I still give you a hug?" he inquired.

I exclaimed, "Dude, I don't care if my ribs were broken, I'm not missing a hug from you."

He smiled and gave me one of his amazing hugs. I've always loved his hugs. He gives the best ones. They've always lifted me up whenever I was down or calmed me whenever I was anxious. They always felt like they were full of love. When we let each other go, I asked, "So how was the drive?"

"The drive wasn't bad. It was waiting for our gear and the rental car that was the pain."

"Oh yeah, that airport can give you such problems sometimes. But I guess all airports can be like that."

Some guy with dirty blonde hair stepped forward and said, "Yeah, tell me about it. That's why we're running a little behind, which I do apologize for. I don't like being late."

"Nah, it's fine. Thankfully, it's been quiet today, so you haven't really missed anything exciting."

We all laughed. Jack then said, "Ashlynn let me introduce you to everybody. This is Chad," pointing to the guy that doesn't like being late, "my producer."

I shook his hand with my good one. I said, "And that would explain why you like to be on time." He nodded and laughed. "It's very nice to meet you, Chad. Sorry for the awkward handshake."

He smirked. "No worries. It's nice to meet you too, Ashlynn."

Jack continued, "And this is Greg," pointing to a guy

with medium-long blonde hair, "my tech guy." I greeted and awkwardly shook his hand as well. "And that's Jerry," pointing behind me to a guy with a video camera in his hand, "my cameraman."

As I turned to meet Jerry, I inquired, "Uh, are you recording right now? Is that why you were hiding behind me?"

He looked away from the lens, nervous. "Yeah, uh…" he acted like a child who got caught doing something he wasn't supposed to be doing.

Jack chimed in, "It's for the show, hon. He's pretty much going to be recording the entire time. I hope that's okay?"

I replied, excitedly, "Yeah, of course. That's totally fine. Jer, please breathe."

He let out a massive breath. We all laughed again. I guess he got scared thinking I was going to lash out and break his camera. I continued, "And please, make yourselves feel at home. I know you guys are probably exhausted from the trip, but I'll get some food ready while…"

They all screamed out, "FOOD," as they grabbed their stuff and ran past Jack and I like we weren't even there.

I laughed as we dodged them. "Um, okay. I guess they're not that exhausted."

Amid picking up his bags and walking toward the cabin, Jack said, "Yeah, they have real big appetites. They could be sleeping and if they smell food, they'll be wide awake in seconds. It costs me more to feed them than to buy equipment for the show."

"Well, it's a good thing I have food in the cabin. You can save some of your budget." I winked.

He chuckled. "Oh, thank you, my savior. It's much appreciated."

Walking into the cabin, I showed the guys where they could put their equipment and where they'll be sleeping. Not too long after, we sat down for a late lunch – just some sandwiches I prepared. But once they heard we would be having BBQ for dinner, they stopped to save room. Chad said, "These sandwiches are delicious, Ash, but I think I can speak for all of us when I say that BBQ is our middle name. I can eat that every day and never get sick of it."

I agreed. "Dude, I'm the exact same way; BBQ all day, every day!"

Jerry said, "Jack, you marry this girl! You marry this girl right now!"

We all laughed while Jack and I turned bright red.

Later in the day – after the guys started setting up some equipment in the cabin – I worked on the side dishes while they were kind enough to do the barbequing. We continued to chat while doing so: learning more about each other, Jack and I catching up, me telling them more about the creature and showing them where I've been seeing it. You know, fun stuff.

Once we finished eating and cleaning up, the guys continued working by putting cameras up around the cabin while Jack and I stayed inside. He went to go grab his tablet. We then sat down at the dining room table across from each other. He explained, "Okay, Ash, I have a program on here where I can recreate the creature once you describe it to me."

"You mean like 'Paint'?"

"Something like that. Now can you tell me more about what it looks like?"

"Yeah, um…" I shuddered a little as I thought about it.

"It's tall, maybe about six or seven feet. Its skin is black and rough, almost like bark."

"Like on a tree?" he asked.

"Exactly. It blended in with the trees. That's why when I first saw it, it took me a minute to see what it actually was."

"Got it. What else?"

"It's very muscular with nails that are like claws on its hands."

"And it's feet?"

"I honestly didn't get a good look at its feet."

"That's okay."

I stopped for a moment to watch Jack doing whatever he was doing on his tablet. He was so focused and so intent on his work. I guess you can say I was fascinated. After a few minutes, he looked up at me and smiled. "What?"

I snapped out of it. "Nothing. I just couldn't help but watch you work. It's mesmerizing."

We continued staring at each other until from behind us we heard, "Aw." We looked to see Jerry with his camera in hand. Our faces once again turned as red as a cooked lobster. Jack said, "Really, Jer?!"

"What? You told me to document everything."

We laughed. Jack said, "Please go finish putting up cameras around the cabin."

"You got it, boss," and left.

Jack continued, "So, Ash what about its face?"

I felt my smile disappear and my face go from red to white as I thought about it. Jack noticed. "Ash, you okay?"

I looked at him and nodded. "It's just, whenever I think about it, especially its face, I get so frightened."

He replied with empathy, "I understand, hon. Please

take your time."

When I answered, my voice shook as I saw flashes of it. "Its eyes are a piercing red-orange color, like fire embers, with rows of sharp teeth in its mouth and short like horns or spikes on its head." I raised my hands up and down above my head, mimicking the spikes.

"How long would you say they are?"

"Uh, a couple of inches I guess."

"Is there hair anywhere?"

"None that I saw."

"Great. Anything else?"

I thought for a moment, still seeing flashes of the abomination. That's when it hit me. "It was wearing something," I replied, sounding confused.

"What, Ash?"

I looked up at him, puzzled. "Thinking back, re-seeing that…thing, I'm realizing it was wearing pants. Kind of like the Hulk, torn and frayed."

"What type of pants? Like jeans?"

"Yeah."

After a few minutes, Jack stared at his tablet in astonishment. "Wow," he said as he covered his mouth. I stared at him. He was very hesitant to show me what he created. "Uh, Ash," he turned his tablet toward me, "is this what you've been seeing?"

I looked and on the screen was a near perfect replica of the creature. I gasped. "Oh my gosh." I couldn't catch my breath. It was like the wind was knocked right out of me. Jack came over, sat next to me, and held me. "It's going to be okay, hon. We'll find out what this thing is, together."

I panned up to him. I said, "Yeah?"

He replied, "Yeah."

We gazed into each other's eyes. For the first time in a *real* long time, I felt comforted. It felt like it was just the two of us, like there was no one else around. His crew was gone. The creature was nowhere in sight. It was just me and him. He caressed my face and I melted into his arms. I was on cloud nine until we heard, "Hey, guys."

We came back to reality. We looked over to see Chad coming into the dining room. He started, "So how did the…" He looked up. "Am I interrupting something?"

"Uh, no," Jack said as we backed away from each other a little. "What's up?"

"I wanted to check and see how the recreation was going?"

Jack replied, "Take a look for yourself," and handed him his tablet.

"Woah!"

"Yeah. This is something the world has never seen before."

"And we're going to be the first to document it," Chad said with excitement.

"Exactly."

Chad then asked me, "Ash, would you mind if we interviewed you? It'll obviously be for the show. We'll just ask you some questions about yourself and the creature."

I replied, "Sure, I wouldn't mind at all. When would you like to do it?"

"Tomorrow, as long as it's sunny out. We really don't have any lighting equipment right now since we're just starting out. We worried more about getting the right cameras than anything else, so it'll be easier for us to work with natural light."

"Yeah, that's perfectly fine with me."

Seconds later, Greg came running in shouting, "Hey, guys! You need to come outside and see this!"

Jack, Chad, and I ran outside to see what it was. As we reached Jerry and Greg, they pointed to the cabin, "Look!"

The wood outside my room was all scratched up. I gasped. Jack held me. I recalled, "I heard it scratching at the cabin last night, but I didn't expect this."

I stared at the marks, realizing I've seen them before. They looked eerily like the ones I saw on the move theater. *Did this thing see me in Nonoma and follow me? Why is it here? What does it want from me?*

****

While lying in bed trying to get some sleep, I heard a knock at my door. I got excited. I quickly got out of bed and walked over to the door. *Please let it be Jack! Please let it be Jack!* I opened it. *It is!*

He smiled and whispered, "Hey."

I beamed. "Hey."

"May I come in?"

"Of course."

He came in and closed the door behind him. "I figured you wouldn't be sleeping."

"Yeah, well I can't stop staring at the wall and thinking about what happened and what we saw."

"Yeah, same here."

"Please, sit." We both went and sat on my bed.

As we did, he said, "I've also been scanning through every resource I know to try and find something that could explain what you're seeing."

"And?"

"Nothing. No urban legend, no Native American folklore. It seems like it came out of nowhere."

"Really? I wonder if that white building has anything to do with it," I pondered.

"It's possible. I would like to go check it out, see what I can find."

"Count me out of that trip. One experience in that building is enough for me."

"Oh, come on, Ash. I'll be there. I'll protect you," he took my hand in his. "You know I would make sure no harm ever comes to you."

I held his hand. "I know."

We continued to stare into each other's eyes. I said, "I know I've said this a million times throughout our life, but I'll be saying it a million more because it's true. I cannot thank you enough, Jack, for everything. You mean the world to me." He smiled. I stuttered, "I mean, what you do for me means the world."

His smile vanished. "Oh, of course. Anytime."

He let go of my hand. My heart dropped. I felt horrible. *Jesus, Ash! We're in our thirties now! Why the hell are you shying away?*

To lighten the mood, Jack said, "Do you remember when we first met as kids?"

"Ha! You're lucky I remember what happened yesterday, never mind what happened when we were little."

"I remember when I first saw you and all I thought was, 'Oh, no! She's a girl! She's gross! She's got cooties!'"

I laughed so hard, I had to cover my mouth as Jack told me to be quiet. We were trying not to wake the others. I replied, "You were the cooties boy?"

He nodded.

"I do remember a boy constantly saying, 'You got cooties,' to me, but for the longest time I thought it was Glen for some reason."

We continued telling stories and quietly laughing until the wee hours of the morning.

SEPTEMBER 30th

At one point, Jack and I must've nodded off because I woke up with him by my side. I smiled. It felt good. It felt right. Moments later, he awoke. He smiled. "Good morning."

I replied, "Good morning."

"Sorry I fell asleep on your bed."

"No worries. I don't mind. I'm just glad I got some sort of sleep."

"True."

We both yawned. He asked, "What time is it," mid-stretch.

I got up and checked my phone. My eyes widened. "Damn, it's past noon."

"Wow. I'm surprised the guys didn't come looking for me."

Maybe they did and then realized where you were and decided to leave you alone! Good!

While getting out of bed, he continued, "Well, I'm going to go get dressed. I guess I'll meet you out there."

"Yup. Sounds good."

Before he walked out the door, I said, "Jack," he turned to me, "thanks for last night. I had a lot of fun, even though I fell asleep. It was something I needed."

"You're welcome, hon. I had fun, too. I'll see you in a little bit."

After getting dressed, I went out to see the guys setting up cameras in the living room. I went up to Chad. "Hey."

He turned. "Hey, Ash."

I asked, "Are we still doing the interview today?" since I noticed clouds in the sky. They weren't the real dark ones that suggested an impending doom might be coming our way, but the sun seemed to be nowhere in sight.

Chad replied, "Probably not. I'm not really liking the trees in the background contrasting with the cloudy weather."

Jack came up from behind us. "So, what's the call, boss?"

Saddened, Chad answered, "We'll wait for the next sunny day. I would rather see the sunshine through them. It would look better."

I wasn't about to let this one slip by. I had to create chaos. "But if we did it *now* while it's cloudy, it would look more ominous. Look at that," pointing to the camera's screen, "it's the perfect setting since we are searching for a monster, you know."

Chad glared at me. "You just had to mess with my vision," he joked.

I laughed. "Listen, if anybody is going to understand your vision and that things need to be perfect, it's me. I'm a producer as well but ask Jack, I'm a ballbuster. It's one of the main reasons I was put on this earth."

Jack nodded his head fiercely.

I then inquired, "May I ask why you guys didn't get lighting equipment?"

Chad responded, "Well, again, we wanted to make sure we had the best cameras from ones with night vision to a thermal camera, which can cost a pretty penny. But we also figured that a lot of the interviews would be done outside with natural light instead of inside."

"We can move the interview outside. That won't bother me."

"And not show off this cabin? Please. The second I saw this inside I knew the interview would happen in here. It's perfect."

I love seeing fellow producers work. It's fascinating. It's also great to know you're not the only perfectionist out in the world.

Throughout the day, the guys kept their eyes on the videos from the cameras around the cabin to see if anything would pop up. An occasional squirrel or rabbit came across the screen, but otherwise it was quiet. *Watch, this thing won't show up at all! I'm going to look like a nut job!*

After dinner, we sat at the dining room table to strategize for the investigation we were about to do. Jack asked, "Are you going to come with us, Ash?"

"I would love to, if you guys don't mind."

Chad replied, "Not at all. It'll be pretty cool to have the person we're helping join us on the hunt."

Once it was dark out, they gathered their equipment to head out. I was walking through the living room when I saw something out the same window I first saw the creature. I walked over to look out. I could see something moving around, but I couldn't tell what it was. Then I saw those damn red eyes right in front of me. I gasped, freezing in place. All I heard was my heart rapidly pounding in my chest and it breathing through the window pane. We stared at each other for what seemed like hours. Then it banged its hand onto the window. I screamed, stepping backward away from it. Jack came running. "What is it, Ash?"

I continued staring at the window. I wasn't seeing the eyes anymore, but I wasn't completely sure it was gone. Jack came over to me and gently grabbed my good arm. I turned toward him. Chad, Greg, and Jerry were right behind him. He asked again, "What happened, hon?"

"That thing...it was just outside that window," I pointed to it.

"What?"

Chad, Greg, and Jerry ran outside to try and find it while Jack stayed with me, asking if I was okay and what exactly I saw. I continued staring out the window, waiting to see those eyes. As the guys returned, Chad said, "Sorry, Ash, but we couldn't find it anywhere. It disappeared."

I sighed, falling gently into Jack. He held me and rubbed my back. I whined, "Why is this happening? Why is it here? What's going on?"

Jack replied, "I don't know, hon, but we're here and we'll figure it out."

I looked up at him and nodded.

Moments later we went outside to begin the investigation. Thankfully, the weather cleared up with a full moon shining brightly through the trees. We created a bonfire to keep us warm as there was a chill in the air. Greg and Jerry went around setting up their video cameras with night-vision and trap cameras. They did it around the camp area, the forest...anywhere they thought we would be able to capture it on film. Jack and Greg took the first shift of going around, examining the area. I inquired what they were going to do. Jack stated that they were pretty much just going around the perimeter of the cabin, listening for any strange noises, and trying to find anything out of the ordinary. They also wanted to put up more cameras deeper into the forest. Jerry went with them as well since he is their cameraman.

Chad and I stayed back at the camp to watch over everything. I sat by the bonfire while he sat at the table with all of the screens to watch over them. We began to chit-chat. "How did you first meet Jack?" he asked.

I turned toward him. "Well, when I was about three or four, Jack and his family moved into the house next to mine. Our parents became friends, which…"

"Made you and Jack friends."

"Exactly. And we're the same age so we went to the same elementary school, middle school, and high school. We were inseparable. We did everything from family parties to going to the movies and the mall together. I mean, you name it, we probably did it. And we were very protective of each other. We watched over each other like family, you know." He nodded. "I mean, if I was ever in trouble at school with a bully, Jack would be there to defend me. If Jack was having problems with classes, I was there to help him with his homework. If either of us had any family problems, we were there to console and comfort each other."

"Did your brother hate him?"

"Oh, did he ever. It was years before Glen would really talk to him and become friendly with him."

I began to think about Glen, reminiscing on how we would fight because of Jack, how he and Jack would get into arguments, and how we made up by playing games, watching movies, or listening to music. I also remembered one of the first times they were friendly to each other. I smiled with tears welling up in my eyes. Then I heard Chad asking me a question, but it sounded muffled. "I'm sorry, Chad," I said as I wiped my eyes, "what did you say?"

"How much older are you compared to Glen?"

"Oh, um…I'm two years older than him."

"I'm sorry, Ash. I didn't mean to upset you."

"No, it's okay. I just really miss him."

He decided to change the subject. "You know Jack has strong feelings for you, right?"

"I know and so do I. Well, toward him I mean."

He chuckled. "Yeah, I kind of figured that. How come you guys didn't pursue?"

I thought about it for a second before I answered. "I don't know. I mean, we constantly weighed-out the pros and cons of dating, and we wanted to, but I guess for the sheer fact that we were young, we were afraid it wouldn't work out and we would never talk to each other again. We decided to wait until we were older and more mature."

"And," he came over and sat next to me, "what happened?"

"Well, after high school we went to different colleges, and we were doing different things in our lives; we unfortunately lost touch. I figured he decided to move on, so I did too. But every guy I dated I either didn't fall in love with or it just didn't feel right."

He nodded.

"Then after college, we began talking again, but he never mentioned anything about us, so I thought that was it. We were just going to be friends, which I'm totally fine with," I said with a hint of uncertainty. I stared into the flames. "As long as he's in my life, I'm happy."

Under his breathe, Chad said, "Yeah, right."

I became defensive. "Excuse me?"

He exclaimed, "Oh, stop hiding from it, Ash! You two are perfect for each other. All he talks about is you."

I beamed. "Really?!"

"Yeah! You'd think you two have been dating for years. I thought you were until he said, 'My *friend*, Ashlynn is coming to visit,' so I questioned him."

"And," I was on the edge of my seat…or log, "what did he say?"

"That he *wants* your relationship to be more, but he doesn't know how to do so. What to do or what to say." My heart fluttered. "You know, he was truly heartbroken when you didn't show up or answer his text. He thought something happened to you or he did something wrong."

I felt like a rug was swept from right underneath me. I went from an all-time high to an all-time low. I remember when Jack and I talked about me and the boys going down to Sacramento to visit for a couple of days. We were both so excited to finally see each other since it's been over a year from when we last hung out. For all I know, our relationship could've started then. But everything happened with the boys, and I completely forgot about him. I felt so terrible. My heart shattered into a million pieces. I sighed, "Shit! I didn't mean…"

"But," Chad stopped me before I said anymore, "when you called him the other day, he lit up so bright, you would've thought he was the new sun."

I brightened up.

"Just like that," he said.

I laughed. *Back on cloud nine, baby!*

That's when we heard them coming toward the camp. Chad leaned forward and, in a slight whisper, said, "I would let him know that you obviously still have strong feelings for him and see what comes of it. It might be the best decision of your life."

"Will do. Thanks, Chad."

He winked at me. As he went back to his "post", Jack, Greg, and Jerry returned. Jack said, "We heard some rustling out there, but we didn't see anything. It could've been just a small animal."

I asked, "So what do we do now?"

Jack shrugged, "Pretty much, we sit and wait for now. We'll go back out in maybe an hour or two to see what we can find then."

And that's exactly what we did. Jack, Chad, Jerry, and I sat by the bonfire while Greg sat at the table watching all of the different screens. Chad kept on looking at me, giving me this eye of "What the hell are you waiting for? Say something!"

I wanted to. I kept on reaching out to grab Jack and talk to him, but I kept on pulling back. I was so nervous. I kept on thinking, *Maybe right now is not the best time! What if he changed his mind? What if Chad's lying?*

Finally, as we were about to hit the two-hour mark, Greg saw something on one of the cameras. "Guys," we turned toward him. He looked at us with fear in his eyes, his skin turning as white as snow. "What the fuck is that?" pointing to one of the screens.

We immediately got up to look. The second I saw it, my heart sank. "That's it." Everyone looked at me. "That's the creature that has been haunting me for the past couple of days."

We stared at the screen, watching it slowly go by, like it knew it was being watched and it was trying to hide. Chad turned to Jack, "Dude, this is it! The holy grail! Let's go after it!"

Jack got pumped. "Alright, guys! This is a code green! Let's go!"

While they gathered their gear, I thought for a second. *I might be scared of this thing, but I have to find out where it's going and what it's doing! Maybe it'll lead me to the boys!*

I gathered up some courage, stepped up, and said, "Why don't I go?"

Stunned, Jack said, "I'm sorry, what?"

"Why don't I go out there and search for it?"

"By yourself?"

Before I could answer, he replied, "Uh, I don't know about that, Ash. I mean this thing seems to be after you and if it gets to you, only God knows what it'll do. It could rip you to shreds or eat you alive or…"

I stopped him, "I get it and thanks for the encouraging thoughts, Jack, but I want to do this." I took his hand in mine. "Please." We gazed into each other's eyes. "I don't have to go out there by myself, but I do want to join you guys, if that's okay."

Once again, it felt like everything stopped for a moment and we were the only two people standing in the middle of the forest. I said, "With you by my side, nothing bad will ever happen to me."

We continued staring at each other as a unanimous "Aw" echoed around us. We jumped away from each other like we got caught by our parents being too close together.

With sincerity, Chad said, "Sorry, guys. Didn't mean to ruin the moment."

Jack replied, "It's fine. We should get to work, anyway. So, uh…yeah, Ash you can join us, just stay close, okay?"

"You got it," I replied as I took my sling off.

"How's your arm?"

"It's feeling a bit stiff, that's why I'm taking it out."

"That's what he said."

"Really, Jack!" We all laughed as I smacked him with my sling.

He turned to Greg, "Are you still seeing it on the screen?"

He looked. "No, now it's gone."

"Shit, I hope we didn't miss it."

Chad directed, "Greg and I will stay back to keep an eye on things. Jer, you'll go with them to record any findings."

Jerry gave him a thumbs up. "Got it, boss."

I asked, "Do you guys have walkies that way if you," pointing to Chad and Greg, "see anything on the screens, you can direct us on which way to go?" They all looked at each other. "What? Were the cameras really that expensive that you couldn't afford walkies?"

Sort of embarrassed, Jack replied, "Honestly, we didn't even think about having those until you mentioned it. We've been mainly using our phones to communicate with each other."

I rubbed my forehead. "Oy."

We grabbed whatever equipment we needed and headed out. My heart was frantically beating. I held onto Jack's hand so hard, I'm surprised he didn't yell at me to lighten up, but he was holding mine just as strong. We walked toward the camera where we had just seen the thing. It took us a little while since it was pretty far into the forest, but as we walked, we searched around for any clues. That's when we found a footprint. Jack was the first to see it. "Holy shit! Look what I found!" he exclaimed.

I looked down. "Oh gosh, not another one."

He looked at me. "You've seen this before, Ashlynn?"

It was weird hearing him say my full name, but I knew it was for the camera. He had to stay somewhat professional. I said, "Yeah, I saw one the other day back here." I leaned in closer. "However, this one looks different. It looks wider than the one I saw."

"Interesting. Do you think there's more than one creature out here?"

My stomach twisted into a knot. "Unfortunately, I'm starting to think that."

He looked up at Jerry. "Jer, can you grab the casting kit for me? I want to take this back with us and show it to a professional to see what they think."

"Sure."

I had to ask while he worked, "Do you think it's Bigfoot?"

He chuckled. "You know, that would be everyone's first assumption as we're in the middle of Washington state and found these footprints, but these aren't from Bigfoot."

I was gob smacked. "Really? How can you tell?"

"It was one of the creatures I did a comprehensive study on in college. All of his footprints are similar. They're human-like but usually have either primate tendencies because of the big toe sticking out, or there's no curves. This, however, has a curve where the arch of your foot is. This definitely comes from a human, it's just gigantic in size."

Once he finished smoothing out the plaster, he cleaned his hands and took out a device.

"What's that?"

"This is a GPS device. I'm able to put the location of the print in it that way, once it dries, we can come back and retrieve it."

"Ah…wait a second. You guys think of buying this, but not of getting walkies?"

Jack glared at me. "Shush."

I glared back at him. He winked at me. I couldn't help but smile. "Fine you win."

From there, Jack began using a thermal imaging camera to see if he could pick up any abnormalities – whether hot or cold – in the area. While scanning he noticed something pretty big on the screen giving off heat. "What the hell is that?" he reacted.

"Do you think it's the creature?" I asked.

"It could be. Or it could be something else. We won't know until we get a little closer." He looked down at me. "Are you sure you want to continue with us? You can stay here. We won't be long. We're just going in a few feet through here," pointing in the direction of the anomaly, "to see if we can figure it out. We'll come right back."

I nodded. "Okay, I'll stay here and wait." Figured it might be easier if I stayed back.

Before leaving me, Jack scanned the area with the thermal camera to make sure there wasn't any other anomalies around me. "You should be safe. If anything, you holler for me or you come running, you got it?"

"I will."

He gently squeezed my hand. "Let's go, Jer."

As I stood there, watching Jack and Jerry walk away from me, I felt like someone was watching me. I shook in terror. At one point, I took the flashlight that was in my hands and scanned the area. Between the flashlight and the full moon illuminating the forest, I was able to see a pretty good distance but found nothing. I began to hear some rustling noises behind me. Probably the same ones Jack was hearing while he was out here. I turned and still saw nothing. I continued to hear the rustling noise just echoing all around me. I took in a couple of deep breathes and said out loud, "Relax, Ash. It's probably just Thumper or Bambi. Let's pray it's not Flower."

I tried composing myself.

A few moments later I heard the same breathing sound from earlier. Then I heard someone – or something – saying, "Ash," in this deep voice. I looked around, whispering, "Hello," when I felt something on my shoulder. I screamed and spun around to find Jack. "Hey, it's me. It's okay."

I took in several deep breathes. "Shit, Jack, you scared me!"

"I'm sorry, hon. Are you okay?" he asked as he caressed my head.

"Yeah, I'm fine." Jack, Jerry, and I started to laugh like we were delirious. You know that "I'm so fucking tired" laugh. Yeah, that one.

After a little bit, I asked, "Did you guys find anything?"

"No, nothing. What about you? It looked like you might've heard or saw something out here."

"Yeah, I did. I heard some rustling sounds and then I heard what sounded like someone or something breathing, and my name being called out."

Jack was baffled. "Your name? Are you sure you heard correctly?"

"I think. I mean I could be wrong, but it sounded like somebody was saying 'Ash.'"

"Well, one of our cameras is around here, so maybe it picked it up. I think we got some pretty good evidence and it's getting late, so why don't we call it and head back to camp."

Jerry and I agreed.

We trekked back to the camp. When we got there, we asked if anything else popped up on the cameras. Greg and Chad were hesitant to share what they saw. "Well…we…there," Greg stuttered.

Jack insisted, "Dude, spit it out!"

"We saw the thing right by you, Ash. It was following you and watching you like a fucking hawk."

"And you didn't contact us because?" Jack was annoyed.

"We tried; it went straight to voicemail."

"Oh, crap! Don't tell me my phone died."

I remarked. "And that's why you need walkies."

Jack glowered at me. I said to Greg, "Can you show me? I want to see."

"Sure." He looked down at his notepad to remind himself of the time he saw it. He went to that exact time and what I saw made my heart drop through my feet and into the very ground I was standing on. Not more than five feet ahead of me was the monster. We all stared in disbelief. Jack asked what I was thinking, "How the hell did you miss that?"

"I don't know," I answered as I scratched my head. We saw it doing something but couldn't tell what exactly. I asked,

"Is there audio with this as well?"

Greg replied, "Yeah, why?"

"Because I heard some noises by me, and I wonder if this thing was…was trying to talk to me."

"Talk to you?" Chad asked.

I looked at him. "Yeah."

They turned on the speakers and turned up the volume. We faintly heard it saying something. That's when Greg looked up at me and said, "Is it saying what I think it's saying?"

"Oh my god," Jack said, "it *is* saying your name."

Tears welled up in my eyes. I turned and ran for the cabin. *How the hell does this thing know my name?*

I ran into my room. Jack wasn't too far behind me. I ran right into his arms. "Oh, Jack! I just had the most terrible thought! What if this thing is Roman? Or Kaden? Oh god, what if it's Glen?"

I cried hysterically. He held me tight and close. He caressed my head as it rested on his chest. It took me sometime to settle down, but Jack stayed with me, doing everything he could to help. "I don't know if that's the case, hon, and I hope it's not, but I promise you, on my life, that we will figure this out, together."

I looked up at him. "Yeah?"

"Yeah," he responded as he gently stroked my cheeks wiping away the tears. My whole body flooded with warmth. That feeling came back of it just being the two of us, my new favorite feeling. *God help anyone who decides to ruin this!*

We gazed into each other's eyes. I said, "You always knew what to say or do to make me happy."

He smiled. "Well, that's because I, uh…" My heart

pounded in my chest. *Say it! Oh, please, say it!* "I love you!"

I smiled so widely I think it went past my ears. I said, "Yeah?"

He beamed. "Yeah!"

"I love you, too." We both leaped in for a kiss and it felt so good! I don't know about him, but I didn't want to stop. This was over twenty years in the making. We had twenty years of kissing to catch up on. But then we heard Chad. "Hey, guys!"

GOD DAMNIT!

We stopped kissing and looked at him. I gave him the strongest death stare ever. I might've even scared away the Grim Reaper with it. I wanted to yell, "Dude, this was your idea and now you're interrupting us?!" but I think our stares at him said it all. He became incredibly uncomfortable. "I am so sorry to, uh," he cleared his throat, "bother you, but I just want to borrow Jack for a hot minute."

I sighed. "Alright, I guess."

I didn't want him to leave and neither did he. He gently grabbed my chin, so I could look up at him. He said, "I'll be right back."

"You better."

He gave me one more kiss before he walked out of the room. Just as Chad was about to follow him, he turned to me and said, "Congratulations. You just made him the happiest man in the world."

"Thanks for the advice."

"Anytime."

Once he left, I sat on my bed, nibbling on my lower lip. I thought, *Oh my gosh, that felt so good! Is this finally happening? Is this really happening?* I pinched myself and felt it. *Yup! This is really happening!*

Not too long after he left, Jack was back. "Is everything okay?" I asked.

"Yeah, they just wanted to tell me what the plan was for the rest of the night into the morning. They're going to take shifts to watch over the cameras to see if it comes back."

"What shift are you taking?"

"I'm not taking one."

"Really?!"

He nodded.

"Then…why don't you join me in bed?"

"Yes, ma'am!" With no hesitation, he jumped in, and we slid underneath the covers.

As we got comfortable, I snuggled up beside him. He even asked, "Is your arm okay?"

I actually forgot all about it. "Um…well, I'm lying on it, completely forgetting I bruised it and so far, it's fine, so…yeah. I think I'm good."

He wrapped his arms around me and held me. I melted into him. *Ah, this feels so right!*

He hinted, "You know, I can't stop thinking about that kiss."

"Would you like a refresher?"

"Oh, stop, please, you're twisting my arm," he joked.

We both roared with laughter, but then kissed. It was just as good as the first time and much longer. I was hoping for something more, but with the guys in the cabin, it would've been a little awkward.

At one point, I asked, "So, are we officially old enough to start a relationship?"

"You might be, but I'll never grow up."

I scowled at him even though I couldn't help but smile and chuckle. "You're such an ass."

"Yes, but I'm *your* ass now."

"Damn right!"

We continued kissing for some time until he said, "Why don't you get some rest, hon? I know you haven't been sleeping well. I'm here and I'm not going anywhere. Plus, we might have a busy day tomorrow if the sun is out. Chad will want to do the interview."

"You want me to go to sleep now? After we officially started our relationship? But I'm too happy!"

Nonetheless, as I laid back down into his arms, he brushed my hair with his fingers and gently pressed his lips against my forehead. I felt so much love and protection that after God knows how long of no sleep, I was able to doze off, naturally, and slept the entire night.

OCTOBER 1st

Waking up this morning in Jack's arms was perfection. I mean, waking up yesterday next to him was one thing but waking up in his arms, knowing we are officially boyfriend/girlfriend, is something I've always dreamed of, but I didn't know if it would ever come to fruition. However, there I was, staring at the man I have loved for so long and I couldn't wait to be with. When he woke up, he smiled and said, "Good morning, my beautiful girlfriend."

"Good morning, my handsome boyfriend."

"Damn, it feels so good to say that and hear it," he said.

The rest of the morning I'm going to keep to myself. He had some "happiness" to take care of and I was more than willing to help. And no, it's not too early. We've known each other for close to thirty years and wanted each other for at least twenty. If anything, it was almost too late. And what's funny is we both forgot that his crew were in the cabin until we walked out – fully clothed – to them clapping and cheering us on. However, instead of being embarrassed, I said, "I hope you guys took notes because he knows how to please a woman."

They roared. "Oh, yeah! Go, Jack!"

After breakfast, Jerry came up to me and asked, "How's your elbow doing? You want me to check it out?"

Jerry is also a certified medic, so that's why he asked. I responded, "Aw, thanks, Jer. If you wouldn't mind, but it's feeling pretty good."

He did a couple of things where I felt a nice little sting. He said, "Yeah, it's going to take some time before that's fully healed but keep on resting it and icing it, and you'll be fine. I'll grab you some ice and your sling."

"Best doc ever."

A few moments later, I went to grab my phone when I noticed Chad lying on the couch. I walked over to him. "Chad?" He opened his eyes. "You okay, bud?"

"Yeah, I'm fine. It's just your food, Ash, is *so* good. I'm contemplating calling up the hotshots at the network and telling them we're staying here. Your food is too good to leave."

I blushed. "Aw, thanks, Chad. But we have stuff to do, so get moving."

"Uh, who's the producer here?"

I laughed out loud. I grabbed my phone and called my parents to tell them about Jack and I. Figured they could use some good news and they were thrilled. They were shouting, "Oh, yeah," "That's great, honey," and, "It's about damn time," over the phone. I think at one point I actually heard them with my own ears that's how loud they were. Then, of course, my dad said, "Put Jack on the phone. I want to talk to him."

I grumbled, "Really, Dad? You're going to have 'the talk' with him? You know Jack."

Even my mom said, "Come on, Bob, it's Jack. We've known him for a long time and knew they would eventually get together."

Well, that's comforting to know even my parents thought Jack and I would end up together!

He insisted, "I know, but still. You're my little girl and I want to make sure you have the best."

I rolled my eyes. "Alright, Dad, hold on."

I went into the dining room. "Jack." He looked up at me. "It's Dad."

His head dropped down. He got up from his chair. "Crap. This is the talk I've always feared to have with your father." I held in my laughter. He took the phone from me. "But I also couldn't wait for it because it meant I was with you," and gave me a kiss.

A unanimous "Aw" echoed from the Greg and Jerry.

We both gave them dirty looks.

As he walked away, he began, "Hello? Hey, Mr. Amu…" He paused. "I'm sorry," he looked at me, "Dad!"

I palmed my forehead. He went into another room to talk privately with my dad while I went and sat down with the guys. A moment later, Chad came rolling in. "So happy you can join us, bud. How's the food baby?"

He rubbed his belly. "Still kicking."

We all laughed. Then Greg said, "I'm guessing your father is one tough dude."

"Nah, he's really a nice guy, just very protective of me. You know I'm his only daughter, his little girl, his princess, so…"

Chad chimed in, "He must interrogate every man that wants to date his daughter to make sure they're right for her."

"Okay, seriously, dude you need to stop doing that or people will start thinking we're the ones who are dating," I responded, playfully.

We all laughed again. Greg said, "No, he does that to all

of us, all the time. It's the creepiest thing." He looked at him. "Do you like read minds or something?"

Chad shrugged. "It's a gift, I guess."

I continued, "But exactly."

"Wait, so how did Jack know about 'the talk'?" Jerry inquired.

"I warned him." Then I asked, "So what's the plan for tonight?"

Chad replied, "Well, first, since the sun is out, we'll finally do the interview."

"Awesome. Your vision can now come to life," I joked.

"Precisely. And then…"

That's when Jack came back. He was relieved. "Well, that wasn't so bad."

"They hung up?" I asked.

"Yeah, why?"

"They didn't want to say goodbye to their daughter?"

"I guess not. They both did say that they love you, though."

"What the hell?!"

Jerry said, "I guess someone has been lowered on the totem pole."

"I know, right?! Damn, that was quick!"

We all roared with laughter. Then, Chad said, "Alright, Jack, you ready to do the interview?"

"Sure. Ash, you good?"

"Yeah, I just want to make one other quick call before we do it."

Chad replied, "That's fine. You can go do that while we get everything ready."

I got up and went over to Jack to retrieve my phone. After he handed it to me and I began walking away, he wrapped his arm around my waist and whispered in my ear, "We already did it, but I'm good to go again."

I bit my lower lip. I whispered back, "Maybe later, if you behave."

He raised his eyebrows and lightly grabbed my butt.

As they went to work turning my living room into an interview room, I decided to call Sheriff MacReedy to apologize for what I said the other night. "It was wrong of me to say. Can you ever forgive me?"

"Oh, Ms. Ashlynn, of course. Yes, what you did say was wrong and I could possibly arrest you for it, but I would never do that to you. You were hurt and angry. I understand."

I actually teared up a little. "Thanks, Sheriff."

"So I guess your friends are helping you figure out what you saw?"

My smile disappeared and the tears stopped rolling. I was utterly stunned. "Excuse me? How did you know I have guests, Sheriff?"

He stammered for his words. "Well, after we spoke, I wanted to check in with you and make sure you were okay, but as I passed by, I saw another car in the driveway, so I figured you had guests."

"Okay, but how did you know they were here to help me with what I saw."

"Oh, sorry, darlin'. I have to go. I've got a lot of work to do. I'll talk to you soon," and then hung up.

I stared at my phone, mouth agape. Jack noticed and came over. "Everything okay?"

I told him what the sheriff said to me. He wasn't as

shocked as I was. "Well, he had to figure you would get someone out here to help you if you stayed."

"I guess. Just the way he asked, though, was really weird and alarming to me."

"True, but he is the sheriff of this small town. He's got to watch out for it and make sure nobody bad is coming in."

I shrugged.

He gently grabbed my shoulders. "Want to hear some good news?"

I looked up at him and smiled. "Sure, what's that?"

"We're about to do our first interview together and it's going to be awesome."

I chuckled.

"You ready?"

"Yup, let's do it."

We began to walk toward the living room, his arm around my shoulders, when he said, "Didn't you say we would do that later?"

I shook my head. "I can't with you."

We both laughed.

As we came up to it, I thought I walked into an episode of *60 Minutes*. There were two steel chairs catty-cornered in the middle of the room spaced about five feet apart from each other with one of my mom's area rugs right beneath them. There were two other chairs in front of them where Jerry and Greg sat with their cameras on tripods to film the interview. The windows were partially covered up by...sheets? Chad came over to me. "You like it?"

"Dude, this is incredible, but...are you using my parents' sheets?"

"Yeah, sorry. I hope that's okay. I didn't want it to be so

bright in here that you guys were drowned out by the light so I MacGyvered it with gaffer's tape and sheets."

I gawked at him. I was impressed, but I needed to check, "That tape is not going to ruin the walls, right?"

"Nah, it shouldn't."

"Okay, good because if it does, you will be dealing with Nancy Amuso and I will pray for your mortal soul."

Chad laughed. Then Jack came over and took my hand. "What do you think?"

"I'm floored."

"Yeah, Chad can be a miracle worker."

We looked at him and he gave us a slight bow. He asked, "Are you guys ready?"

Jack panned to me. "Ash?"

"Ready whenever you are."

Chad said, "Alright, it's show time."

Jack and I went and sat down in our respective seats. We went over a couple of things before he reminded me, "Just act natural, hon. You'll be fine. And also remember, the audience doesn't know we know each other, so answer each question like it's the first time we're meeting."

I nodded and thought to myself, *Yeah, if they only knew!* I then inquired, "Why are there two cameras, babe?"

Jack was rubbing his forehead while reading his note-cards – his way of expressing stress and nervousness. It took him a bit before he said, "I'm sorry, what, hon?"

I repeated my question. "Oh, because one is on you, and one is on me. When it comes to post-production, it'll be easier to cut back and forth than if we just had one camera moving back and forth. It'll look cleaner."

"Ah, makes sense. But what if I wanted to make a weird

face at you? Would that camera," pointing to the one facing me that Greg was controlling, "capture it?"

"Yes, however, we can edit it out."

I rubbed my hands together and cackled, "Ha! It's time to have some fun!"

He gave me that handsome, loving smile of his, shook his head, and sighed. "This interview is going to be interesting."

As the guys finished up – making sure the lighting was right, the angles were right, etc. – I glanced over to the window where I encountered the creature yesterday. I began reliving that moment: seeing it standing right in front of me, its eyes boring a hole into me, it winking at me. *Wait...it winked at me?*

Then I felt a light touch on my arm and heard Jack saying, "Ash?"

I quickly turned back to him. "You okay, hon?"

"Yeah, sorry. I was just in deep thought."

"No worries. You still want to do this?"

I replied, "Of course."

He smiled and nodded. He then looked at Chad, "You guys ready?"

He responded, "I think we are so...action."

With note cards in his hands, Jack took in a deep breath and began. "Hello, everyone and welcome to another episode of *Searching for the Truth*. I am your host, Jack Graives. Right now, I am in the beautiful but quiet town of Lake Minnetaha, Washington searching for a creature that is completely unknown."

I sat in my chair in awe as I watched him work. I was going to make faces at him, but I was completely enamored by him doing his job. I thought, *Damn, this is hot!*

"You will not find it any books since its first sighting happened only a couple of days ago, and I am sitting with the person who saw it. Ladies and gentlemen, please welcome, Ashlynn Amuso."

He turned to me and said, "Ashlynn, thank you for having us in your beautiful home."

"It's my pleasure, Jack."

"How did you find this place?"

"Well, it was really my parents who found it. When I was little, maybe about five or six years old, my parents decided we needed to get away and my father heard about Lake Minnetaha from a co-worker. I don't remember how he found this cabin, but every year we continued to come up to it for our family vacation. The original owner saw how much we loved it, how well we took care of it, and was getting up there in age, so he decided to sell it to us. He told us it would be one less thing for him to worry about."

"That's great. Now how come you're up here, Ashlynn?"

I explained, "My friends, my brother, and I came here for our vacation."

"Cool. Other than your brother being your brother, how did you get to know your friends?"

"We all work for a company called *Replay*."

"Which is?"

"An entertainment company based in New York. We recreate movies, plays, musicals, and concerts for people's enjoyment. We're often called 'the cover band of the entertainment world'."

"And your brother works there, as well?"

"Yup. We all started around the same time."

"What do you guys do there?"

"Well, my friends, Kaden and Roman, are the performers. They act, they sing, they dance, they do it all. Glen and I are more behind the scenes. He designs all the sets and makes all the props while I decide what show we are going to do next, make sure the performers have all their materials. I pretty much make sure everything runs smoothly."

"And how did you all get to know each other?"

I reminisced, "Like I said, we all started around the same time and throughout the first year of us being there, Kaden and Roman came up to me, separately, wanting to date me. I turned them down, though. I mean, they're both very handsome and nice guys, but I wasn't looking for a relationship at the time." Jack winked at me. I smiled broadly. "But after that, we all became close friends. We got together for every holiday like Christmas, New Years, Thanksgiving, Fourth of July…really any holiday where you can get together to celebrate, we did."

Jack interrupted me, "So that's why there were times I offered to fly you out to California for the holidays and you said you couldn't."

I laughed so hard. "Exactly, but I thought we needed to act like we didn't know each other."

"We can edit this part out."

We all roared in amusement. After a moment of composing ourselves, I asked, "What the hell were we talking about?"

Chad reminded me. "Oh, yeah. Okay, so, to go back to what I was saying, we would celebrate every holiday together. We normally met up at my apartment and just have an amazing time. We even went out to different restaurants and bars when we could for some drinks and dinner. We became known as 'The Replay Foursome'. We went everywhere and did everything together. We even created ways of saying hello to each other at work when we didn't have the time to stop and do so. Like Roman and I would wink at each other, since he's the flirtatious one."

Jack grimaced. He didn't like hearing that. Then I stopped and thought for a second. I said out loud, "He winked. It winked." My eyes widened. "Oh my gosh, it did wink at me," once again recalling last night.

"Ashlynn? Is everything okay?"

Tears filled my eyes as I snapped out of it. "I'm sorry, guys, I need a second."

I got up and walked away. Jack followed me. "Hey, baby, what happened?"

"It winked at me, Jack. That thing winked at me last night like Roman used to," I said in distress.

He grabbed a hold of me and pulled me in close. "Sh…it's okay, hon, it's okay." After a few moments, he said, "We can stop the interview if you want."

"No, I'm fine. That just hit me like a Mack fucking truck."

"I know and like I said last night, we'll figure this all out together."

He gave me one more big hug and kiss before we went back. The guys were kind enough to check on me as we walked back in, offering me water and all the time I needed before we started again. It took me a little while, but I was able to continue. "With Kaden, we would nod to each other since he's the laid back one. And Glen and I would give each other the peace sign," as I demonstrated it like no one has ever seen it before.

"So, in other words, you guys were close."

I laughed. "Yes, to make a long story short."

He looked down at his cards. "Um…so…"

He was hesitant in asking the next question. "I was going to ask you, hon, where they are and why they aren't here, but I don't want to upset you any more than…"

I interjected. "No, it's okay, Jack. Do what you have to do? I just can't guarantee that I won't cry."

Chad said, "We have tissues, Ash, if you need them."

"There you go, reading my mind, Chad."

"Like I said, it's a gift."

Jack asked and I answered, through tears. I talked about the day they left and the events leading up to them leaving. Jack was kind enough to mention that if anyone knew any information about them to call their number or e-mail them. From there he started asking me a series of questions about the creature: when I first saw it, to describe it to him, etc. He held up the picture he created on his tablet to show people what it looks like. I was still taken aback by how accurate it looked. Jack glanced at it. "Wow. I hope you don't mind me asking, Ashlynn, but after seeing this why did you stay here? Why didn't you pack your bags and leave? Why did you call us?"

"Because I wanted to make sure I wasn't going completely insane. That I wasn't just seeing things or making things up in my mind. I've been out here for so long, primarily by myself, that I thought I was developing cabin fever or something like that. But when you guys saw it yesterday with me, I was relieved to know that my horror-filled mind wasn't playing tricks on me."

With that, the interview stopped. Chad said, "That's the perfect place to end it. Thanks, Ashlynn."

"My pleasure, guys."

The rest of the afternoon and evening consisted of us keeping a close eye on the cameras. At one point, I thought I saw something running at the peak of the hill, but nothing was caught on tape. As day turned into night and we were getting ready to go outside to continue our search, I pulled Jack to the side. "Can I talk to you for a second?"

"Sure, hon. What's up?"

We went into my room. I closed the door behind us. Jack teased, "Babe, I don't know how good I am with quickies. I like to take my time."

I smirked. "Yeah, I'm not a big fan of them either, but that's not why I brought you in here."

"What's wrong?" He could tell something was weighing on me.

"Jack…I want to go out there by myself tonight."

He snapped, "What?"

"I want to go out into the woods by myself to investigate."

"Yeah, no that's not happening."

"Uh, actually it is."

He became infuriated. "Why the hell would you want to go out there by yourself, Ash? If you find this thing, it could kill you!"

"But what if I'm right, Jack?"

"About what?"

"About this thing being Glen or Kaden or Roman. Jack, ever since I saw it, it hasn't attacked me. When I saw it outside the window the first time, it could've easily broken in to get me, but it didn't. When I was walking around back there," pointing to the backyard, "it could've easily grabbed me, but it didn't. It could've came after us last night, but…"

"It didn't, I get the point."

"Good, so then we're in agreeance."

"Kind of, not really. I do agree with you that this thing could be one of them. I don't agree with you that you are going out there by yourself tonight."

Then my New York bitch came out. "Well, too damn bad because I'm going out there with or without consent. I don't need you to tell me what I can and can't do."

Jack waved his hands in the air. "Then why did you ask me in the first place?!"

"I didn't!" I exclaimed, folding my arms.

We stood in silence for a while. Jack then released a breath and said, "Look, I'm sorry, babe. I just…I don't want us to finally start our relationship and then I lose you."

I unfolded my arms and relaxed. "I know and I'm sorry too. I just want to get all of this figured out."

"I know, babe." He opened his arms wide. I smiled and jumped right into them. He said, "I love you."

"I love you, too."

"Yeah?"

"Yeah."

We kissed. He put me down. "So, this was our first fight as a couple."

"Yup and it's kind of a good thing we've known each other for so long and know how we can be."

"True. But you know what else that means?"

I looked at him. "What?"

"Awesome makeup sex."

I shook my head while laughing. "Have you been holding back on sex until now?"

"No, not really. You?"

"Nope," and walked away.

"Wait, babe, how many?"

"So not having this discussion right now."

****

By nine o'clock, we were outside; the equipment was all set, ready for anything to happen. Jack and I went out first while Chad and Greg stayed back at camp, watching over the cameras. Jerry stayed back, as well, to give us some privacy. "Not every single second needs to be recorded by a 'regular camera'," he said. "The FLIR records too, so we can use that. Just promise me you won't find a monster out there without me."

"We'll try our best," I said.

Jack was carrying the thermal camera in one hand and holding mine in the other. After walking around for some time, I asked, "Picking up any heat there, babe?"

He positioned the camera on me. "Oh, yeah, baby, you're superhot tonight."

"Ha…ha…very funny. I'm talking about out in the woods, smartass."

He chuckled. "Nah, nothing yet."

"I guess that's something else that can be edited out, huh?"

"Yeah, I'm really making Jerry and Greg work."

After a moment of silence, I said, "Jack?"

"Yeah, babe."

"Just to clarify, you know I'll be coming back out here by myself tonight, right?"

He still wasn't too keen on the idea, but calmly replied, "Yes, I know you are."

I gently squeezed his hand, "Thanks, Jack."

"Of course, baby," and gave me a kiss.

We continued our trek through the woods, hand in hand, for another half hour or so. With nothing unusual showing up on the thermal and us not hearing anything out of the ordinary, we decided to head back to camp. Upon returning we asked, "Did you guys see anything on the cameras?"

Greg shook his head.

Around midnight is when I went back out to search for the creature on my own. Greg handed me one of the cameras. He said, "You're all set, Ash. We won't be able to hear and see you with this camera, but we have all of the other cameras out there that can, so we'll still be able to watch over you. Night vision is already on, so use this screen," pointing to the camera's screen, "as your eyes. I don't think you're going to have much luck with light tonight."

I agreed as we both looked up at the sky. The moon might've been full, but the sky was not clear. "Thanks, Greg."

"No problem. Be careful out there."

Both Jerry and Chad said the same thing before I turned to face the forest. That's when I felt an arm wrap around my shoulders. I grabbed it and pulled myself tight into Jack. Then I turned and we looked into each other's eyes. "You come back to me, okay."

I nodded. "You're stuck with me now, babe. I'm not going anywhere."

He smiled. "Good. Try not to wander too far and if

something doesn't feel right, you come right back, understand?"

"I will."

We kissed. I began walking backwards into the woods, staring at the man I love. We both said "I love you" to each other before I turned to start my journey. I tried not to wander too far from camp, but when all you're doing is walking through the woods, looking at a small camera screen, you kind of forget where you are. At one point, I stopped to see the fire from camp was a little speck among the trees.

"Shit! I roamed too far. If we had freaking walkies maybe I wouldn't have because someone would've warned me, but no!" I shouted, making sure they heard me.

Since I felt myself climbing up, I figured I must've started scaling the hill. That's when I started hearing what sounded like footsteps coming toward me. *Alright, Ash! It's time! Let's find out if it's them or not!*

With whatever courage I had, I yelled out, "Whoever you are, step out, so I can see you!"

I stood still, panning around trying to see if anything was coming toward me. At that moment, everything was utterly quiet.

"Glen!" Nothing.

"Roman!" Still nothing.

"Kaden!" Still nothing!

I stayed for a little while longer before deciding to head back to the camp area. While walking back, I screamed, "Fine, you coward! Stay hiding! But eventually, you will have to show yourself!"

Then I heard the footsteps again and the same breathing sound that I heard the other night coming from behind me. I turned to see it clear as day on the camera screen. I still jumped a little, I mean it is scary as hell. I looked up from the screen and all I saw was a black figure and those piercing red eyes. We continued to stare at each other for a little while before I said, "I…I know who you are." It stared at me making what sounded like a growling sound. "It's you, Glen, right?"

It shook its head.

"Okay, then, Roman it's got to be you. You winked at me last night, remember?"

It did it again. My heart raced and my eyes widened. "Shit," I said under my breath. "Then it's got to be you, Kaden. My best friend. My brother from another…mother." Before I could finish the sentence, that damn thing was shaking its head with a smirk on its face. Even in the darkness, I was able to see its mouth curling up.

"Oh, shit!" I yelled out.

It roared.

I screamed, "Jack!"

I turned and ran. I could hear it thudding behind me. I looked down at the screen on the camera and tried to use it as my eyes, but it was extremely difficult to be running and looking at that damn screen at the same time. I ran, trying not to trip over any roots. I was doing well until I stumbled, falling right onto my face and tossing the camera. I tried getting up as quickly as I could, but the creature came up from behind me, grabbed my leg, and pulled me away. I screamed. I attempted to kick its hand as hard as I could, hoping I would hurt it enough to let me go, but to no avail. Instead, it held on tighter. It felt like my ankle was breaking. I still fought, though, as I grew weaker.

While I was being dragged across the forest floor, I felt a thick branch pass underneath me. When I felt it by my hands, I grabbed it and swung it as hard as I could. I hit its arm, which forced it to release me from its grip. As I tried standing up, it rushed at me. I swung again and broke the branch over its head. I knocked it out. Breathing heavily, with so much pain in my ankle – and once again in my elbow – I tried standing up to make my way back to the camp, but I could barely do so. I grabbed my ankle and felt a lot of wetness. I lifted my hand and smelt blood. "Oh, god," I cried.

That's when I felt these massive arms wrap around my waist. I heard, in a low, raspy voice, someone say, "Don't worry, Ash. I got you, hon."

I looked over. "Jack?"

My vision was a little blurry. I don't know if it was from blood loss or if I was in that much pain, but all I saw was this gigantic black figure next to me. It took my arm and wrapped it around what I think was its neck to carry me along, but its skin didn't feel smooth like normal skin. It felt harsher and rougher, almost like there were scabs all over. I looked back and kind of saw two other figures standing over the monster. Whoever was carrying me said, "Don't look back, hon. It's always better to look forward."

"Kaden?"

I could see the fire from camp getting bigger and brighter as we got closer. All of a sudden, he stopped. "You should be okay from here."

He gently laid me against a tree. "I'll watch you from afar to make sure you're safe."

"Kaden!"

He walked away from me. "Please, Kaden, don't go!"

Then I heard Jack screaming, "Ashlynn!"

I screamed out, "Jack!"

I tried to limp toward the camp, but I stepped off on my bad leg and screamed in pain.

"Ashlynn, where are you?"

"I'm over here!"

I regained myself and tried to limp as much as I could. Luckily, it didn't take them long to find me. "Jack!" I fell right into his arms.

He hugged me. "I got you, baby, I got you. Are you okay?"

"No, it's my leg. I can barely stand on it."

Jerry said, "Let's get her back to the campsite, so I can check it out."

Jack picked me up and carried me the rest of the way. He placed me on the ground by the campfire and sat behind me as Jerry checked out my leg. At first, all we saw was blood. My shoes and the bottom of my pants were covered in it. Jerry carefully removed my sneaker and sock. Then he slowly rolled up my pants to reveal the mess that was my ankle. Disturbed, Jerry commented, "Holy shit, Ash! These gashes look pretty deep. You could've lost a lot of blood. You're lucky you didn't pass out from it."

I replied, "I just might. My vision isn't too clear, and I feel so weak."

"Ash, I need you to stay with me okay. Can you tell me what happened?"

"Something attacked me. It dragged me across the forest floor. I fought back, but it kept on tightening its grip."

"That would explain these gashes. Keep on talking to me, Ash. What else happened?" he asked as he pushed on certain areas on my foot and ankle. I was about to answer him when he touched a spot that sent shooting pain throughout my body. I jumped and screamed. He apologized, "Sorry, Ash. Just checking to see if anything is broken."

"Is it? Because that fucking hurt!"

"No, I don't feel any bones sticking out, but that doesn't mean you're completely in the clear. Come on, let's get you inside so I can properly examine it, clean it, and dress it."

Jack picked me up and brought me inside. My vision had cleared, and I was pretty much wide awake after that excruciating pain ran through me. It was like somebody poured a bucket of ice-cold water on me.

They brought me into the kitchen. Jack placed me on the counter, so I could put my foot into the sink. Jerry took another look at it under a brighter light. Even Jack could see it now. He cried, "Jesus Christ, Ash."

Jerry rolled up my pant leg even further to see how far the scratches went. They only went up a little past my ankle, which was the worst. It looked like it went through a meat grinder. Jerry explained, "Okay, Ash, I'm going to continue pushing down on certain spots of your ankle. Tell me if it hurts or not."

"Oh, trust me, you'll know."

With Jack standing beside me, holding my hand, every touch was unbearable. I cringed, holding onto Jack's hand so tight, I could've broken it. He wasn't going to tell me that, though. Jerry then said, "Alright, the good news is," he looked up and saw my face. "Holy shit, Ash! You have scratches on your face too!"

"That could've been from when I fell or when I was being dragged."

"Hold on, I'm going to grab some washcloths and towels, so I can clean you up."

Jack then grabbed my chin and gently pulled my face toward him to look. The utter fear and concern in his eyes made my heart break. Seconds later, Jerry was back. "Here let's take your jacket off as well. See if there's anything on your arms." Thankfully, there was nothing. He asked, "How's the elbow?"

"It flippin' hurts, Jer."

As he went to work wetting the washcloths and cleaning me up, he said, "Okay, so what I was about to say before was it doesn't seem like you have a compound fracture, meaning..."

"My mom was a paramedic, Jer, I know what a compound fracture is."

"Well fuck me then." I half-heartedly laughed as the pain continued to vibrate throughout my body. He continued, "But the bad news is, you could have a non-displaced fracture."

"Great. And how's my face looking?"

He stopped cleaning it. "It's fine. Just some minor scratches."

"So a bruised elbow, a fractured ankle, and a scratched up face. Awesome. What the hell else is going to happen to me?"

Jack immediately replied, "Nothing else will happen; I'll make sure of that."

I looked up at him as he kissed me on my forehead saying, "I got you, baby."

I turned back to Jerry and asked, "So what's next?"

"First, I want to elevate it to help with the pain. Let me go grab one of the equipment boxes. Give me one second."

He ran to his room. Jack stayed with me, continuing to rub my back as I laid my head on his chest. Not too long after he left, Jerry was back with a small box. He said, "Alright let's slowly lift your leg," which hurt like hell, "and lay it right…there. How does that feel, Ash?"

"Okay, I guess."

"Alright, now I'm going to clean your ankle and leg, stitch up any deep cuts you have, and bandage it up."

I nodded. Slowly and methodically – as not to cause any more pain – he cleaned up my ankle. There were a couple of deep wounds that needed stitches, but it wasn't as bad as we originally thought. I think all of the blood surrounding it made it look worse. Then he bandaged up the stitches and wrapped up my ankle in gauze. Lastly, he wrapped my foot and ankle with an ace bandage. He said, "I don't have a boot to give you, but I did wrap it to keep it from moving. I don't want you stepping on that foot until we get you a boot or we're able to properly cast it. Do you by any chance have crutches here?"

"I don't."

Jack said, "Don't worry, babe, I'll be your crutch. I'll carry you wherever you need to go."

I smiled at him and caressed his cheek.

"Okay, you guys are going to be that cute couple that people love and hate at the same time, huh?" Jerry said.

We both shrugged. "Probably," and laughed.

Jerry continued, "I would also like to get some X-rays done to confirm my suspicions. Is there a doctor nearby that can do that?"

"Yeah, Dr. Park. He's about a half hour away from here."

"Okay, cool. I'll take you there tomorrow. Otherwise, keep it elevated and put some ice on it for a little while to help with the swelling and pain."

"Sounds good, doc."

"Alright, now I'm just going to put Band-Aids on some of the scratches on your face, since they're not too bad, and then take a look at your elbow."

He put two bandages on my face and then examined my elbow. As he did, I realized, "Oh, shit, we need to report this to the sheriff!"

Jerry replied, "Don't worry, Ash. Once I'm done, I'll give him a call. Just give me his number. I know how to talk to cops."

I looked at him. "I don't know if I should see that as a good thing or a bad thing, Jer."

He laughed. After examining my elbow – which didn't hurt as much as my ankle, but was still nagging at me – he said, "Okay, good. It doesn't seem like you did any more damage to that."

"Awesome." Then I remembered, "God damnit, the camera!"

Jack retorted, "Don't worry about it, hon. You're far more important. We can look for it tomorrow."

Once Jerry was finished, Jack picked me up, helped me take a bath to get the dirt off of me, dressed me, and put me in bed to rest. Jerry put some pillows under my foot to elevate it and then a bag of ice. "You're all set. Would you like a pain killer to help get some sleep tonight?"

"Oh, I would *love* one."

"You got it. I'll be right back."

Jack grabbed a chair, so he could sit down next to me. Weakly, I asked, "Why don't you join me in bed?"

"Because you deserve the bed to yourself after what you went through." *God I love you!* "How you doing, baby," he asked as he stroked my forehead.

"Well...I'm in a tremendous amount of pain, but otherwise I'm fine."

"Do you want anything? Advil? Tylenol? A stiff drink? Morphine?"

"Oh, the last two sound great right now, but Jerry is grabbing me a pain killer and having you by my side is truly all I need."

He beamed. "Good answer."

Jerry came in with the pill and some water. I took it. He said, "Pretty soon you'll be knocked out, so have fun."

"Thanks, doc. Did you call the sheriff?"

"I tried both numbers you gave me, but no answer. I just left messages, so we'll see."

"It is the middle of the night."

"That's true. Good night, Ash."

"Night."

He let Jack and I be. After a moment, Jack said, "Ash...I honestly thought I lost you. Seeing you being dragged away and reaching out for help. Then the camera out there died and all I heard were your screams. Once those stopped I...I thought the worst."

He began to tear up, which made me tear up. As I caressed his face, wiping away his tears, I said, "Jack, I'm so sorry. That's the last thing I ever wanted you to imagine. I was so stupid to think that thing was them. Or even if it was that it wouldn't attack me."

"That wasn't stupid at all. What I didn't agree with was you risking your life to do so."

"Well, if anything ever happened to me, whether we were just friends or in a relationship, wouldn't you have done the same?" With no hesitation, he agreed. "But here's what's weird. As I tried to get away from it after I knocked it out…"

Jack cut me short, "Wait, you knocked that thing out?"

"Yeah. How do you think I got away from it? Asked it politely to let me go and it did?"

He gave me such a dirty look. "Ha. Ha. But how?"

"I was able to grab a branch, swung at it, and hit it." Jack was impressed. "But someone helped me back to the camp and I think it was Kaden."

"Why do you think that, babe?"

"Because he was talking some philosophical babble to me and that was Kaden. He would always say something to help me understand or make me feel better."

"So then why are you questioning it? And why didn't he help you all the way back to the camp? Show himself to us?"

As he asked question after question, I could feel myself slipping deeper and deeper into sleep. Jack saw. He whispered in my ear, "I'm sorry, baby. We'll talk more tomorrow. I love you."

I think I muffled, "I love you, too," before I fully fell asleep.

OCTOBER 2nd

This morning, I woke up to see Jack contorted in the chair. *Aw, my poor baby!*

I wanted to get up and wake him, but I was immobile. As I huffed and puffed, he awoke. "Hey, baby."

"Morning, love."

He came over to me yawning and stretching. "You okay?"

"Yeah, I wanted to get up, wake you, and be cute, but I can't," gesturing to my leg.

"Aw, babe, it's okay," he helped me sit up. "You're cute no matter what."

We kissed. "Thanks. By the way, how the hell did you sleep in that," pointing to the chair.

He sat next to me on my bed. "Please, that was like a king-size bed for me. While traveling for this show, I've been sleeping in cramped trains and the smallest airplane seats you can imagine."

"Aw, my poor man," I rubbed his back. "And I'm sorry, Jack. I heard you asking me questions last night, but then the pain killer kicked in and you became the adults in Charlie Brown." He imitated the noise. "Exactly. What were you saying?"

"Oh, I, uh…" He thought for a moment. "I was wondering why you were questioning if it was Kaden who helped you out."

"Well because when I looked over to see who picked me up, as I thought it was you, all I saw was this black figure. My vision was a little blurry from…well, you know." He nodded. "I didn't see any features at all. And he seemed massive, but Kaden isn't a big guy. And his skin felt weird. It was rough, not smooth. And his voice was different."

"Interesting."

"Yeah. Seriously, Jack, what the hell is going on here? I mean, I have creatures saying my name. I go out looking for it thinking I know who it is to only get attacked, but then I am saved by something or someone who I think is Kaden," I grabbed my head, "I'm just so lost."

He rubbed my back. That's when there was a knock on the door.

"Hey, guys, it's Chad. May I come in?"

I replied, "Yeah, it's fine."

He didn't open the door. "Are you guys decent?"

"Really?!" Jack replied.

Chad opened the door and walked in. "Hey, I'm just making sure." We laughed. He continued, "I just wanted to let you guys know that we kept watching the cameras over-night but saw nothing out of the ordinary."

Jack said, "Sounds good. Thanks, Chad. Did you guys change the battery on the one that went out last night?"

"No, not yet. We wanted to wait until there was light after what…" He looked at me. "After what happened to you last night, we didn't want to risk it."

Jack understood.

Chad then asked, "How are you feeling, Ash?"

"Eh. I have a fractured ankle, a bruised elbow, scratches all over, and a mind racing with everything that's going on. I'm just peachy."

"Sounds like it. You want anything? Tea? Water? Food?"

"Food and tea sound great."

"You got it. I'll bring it in here, if you want."

"Nah, I'll get dressed and meet you guys out there."

"Sounds good."

Jack helped me change and carried me to the dining room. As we walked in, both Jerry and Greg shouted, "Hey, it's the monster slayer!"

I looked at them like they had a thousand heads. "Okay, am I missing something?"

Jerry said, "When I went back into your room to check in, Jack told me how you took out the monster to get away. You're a badass, girl!"

Jack placed me on one of the chairs. I cautioned, "And don't you forget it."

"Oh, damn!" Jerry laughed.

"Did you knock it out cold?" Greg asked.

"I guess. I mean, it laid there long enough for me to get away."

"I wonder if there's a body. Maybe we should go check it out," Chad said.

Greg responded, "Yeah, and I can change the battery in that camera."

I commented, "I think this a great idea. Let's go."

"Uh, no girl. I'm taking you to the doctors to get that ankle X- rayed and get a proper boot for you," Jerry responded.

"We can go afterwards, doc."

Chad said, "Ashlynn, honestly after last night and in your condition…"

Jack stopped him, "No, guys, let her join us. Not only are we searching for this creature, but we are trying to help her find her family, as well. I'll take care of her. She is my girlfriend, you know," he looked at me and we smiled at each other.

"Oh, jeez! You guys are just going to rub that in now,

huh?"

We both answered, "Yup."

Jerry said, "Alright, but promise me we'll go to the doctor's afterwards."

I held up three fingers. "Scouts honor."

"You were never a girl scout." Jack just had to open his big mouth.

"Shut up."

After eating some breakfast (because God forbid these guys go without eating, which astounds me that they're able to eat so much but be as thin as toothpicks; I eat like that and I bloat up like a balloon), we went out to the backyard. I tried retracing my steps. It was hard, though, since I didn't really see where I was going last night. I was also moving extremely slow with my foot, but Jack was right by my side helping me out. After a long time of wandering around, we finally found the camera. Right by it was the trail from where I had been dragged. As we followed it, we came to the end and found a pool of dried blood. My eyes widened. *Holy shit! I hit it hard enough to make it bleed? Awesome!*

Jack turned to his producer, "Hey, Chad."

"Yeah."

"Do you think the scientists at the institution will be able to obtain DNA from the blood even though it's been dried into the dirt?"

He thought for a second. "I don't see why not. I mean, they've been able to do it from bark. Why not from dirt?"

"Great. Greg, could you grab the kit out of my bag? We'll pick some of this up and send it off to them."

"Sure," Greg said as he unzipped Jack's backpack to find it.

Efficiently, Jack gathered a bit of the dirt with the blood on it and packed it away. At first, I was watching him work, impressed and in awe of seeing my man practice his craft. However, soon after I began to look around to see where it could've been taking me. Ahead of us was the hill that the living room faces where I think I've seen it run up and disappear before. "Hey, guys," I said.

Everybody turned to look at me. "Once you're done, can we go check out that hill?"

Jack replied, "Sure, hon. Why?"

"Because I think we might be able to find something there."

The second Jack helped me up, we started hearing what sounded like gunshots echoing from beyond the hill. "Did you guys hear that?" I asked.

"Loud and clear," Chad replied.

We stood still listening. The gunshots came over in spirts. They weren't rifle shots like someone was hunting; one and done. It sounded more like a fully automatic. I have an uncle who's a gun enthusiast, so we learned about them. *Who the hell is shooting a fully automatic out here?* I thought.

Jack said, "It sounds like they're not too close."

"Yeah, but they're not too far either," I responded.

Then we started hearing roaring sounds and people screaming.

"Shit, that's not good."

That's when we heard roars coming from right over the hill. I said, "Guys, we need to get the hell out of here, go report this to the sheriff."

Jack agreed. "Let's go guys. Everybody in the car."

Jack picked me up. We walked back to the cabin as quickly as we could, heading straight for the rental car. I looked back up toward the hill to see three creatures standing there, watching us. "Holy shit! Guys look!"

Everybody turned. They all gasped. We stood still as if

it was a T- rex in front of us – if we didn't move maybe they would go away. I stared at them, studying them. They were all different in a way. They were all these gigantic beings with spikes for "hair", sharp teeth, and those fire red eyes staring us down, but one's chest was broader than the others. One had arms that were as big as tree trunks. And one was just a little smaller – height and built wise – than the others. As I stared at them, I saw flashes of Glen, Roman, and Kaden. It was like I was seeing them, but I wasn't. Jack muttered, "Everybody slowly get into the car. We don't want to make any sudden moves to cause them to attack us."

We did as he said. They got me in first and then everyone else filed in one by one with Jack being last. I continued to watch them as we drove away from the cabin. Just before I couldn't see them any longer, they turned and ran in the same direction we were going. I tried to find them in the forest as we went along, but I couldn't see anything. I said, "Be careful, guys. They might be following us."

"So do we still go to the sheriff's office?" Chad inquired.

"Yeah, we need to report what's been going on; report what we just heard. Something isn't right. Maybe he knows something," I replied, feeling uneasy. Not like I was going to be sick, but that something bad was about to happen.

****

In no time, we were there. Jack and Jerry helped me out of the car and into the building. As we entered the office, Sheriff MacReedy stood from his desk, saw it was me, and said, "Oh, Ms. Ashlynn! It's so great to…" Then he saw my arm bandaged up and me being helped in. His eyes widened. He came around the counter. "My God, child! What happened?"

"Well, the true question is, are you going to believe me

when I say that I was attacked by a monster last night? The same one *you* questioned me about."

He gasped. "You mean one of those things attacked you?"

We all looked at each other. I replied, "So you *do* know about the creatures!"

His face went from being "oh, crap, I messed up" to "alright, you got me" within seconds. "Please, come around and have a seat. I'll explain everything."

He brought us around the counter to his desk. He pulled out a chair for me. I shouted, "Sheriff, you need to tell me what's going on!"

He held up his hands. "Now calm down, Ms. Ashlynn. Don't get your breeches all tangled up. I said I was going to explain everything." Then he looked up at Jack, Chad, Greg, and Jerry. He said, "But before I do, would you mind introducing me to these fine gentlemen behind you? These must be your friends that came to your rescue."

It was almost like he was salivating as he stared at them. I was a little freaked out and really confused. I snapped my fingers at him. "Sheriff, it's not about them. It's about the creature that I saw and…"

"Creatures," Sheriff MacReedy interrupted me.

"Excuse me?"

"Creatures, Ms. Ashlynn. It's not just one, it's more than one."

"Yeah, I've gathered. You really need to start explaining to me what the hell is going on around here."

He sighed. "You see…"

That's when we heard something outside clawing at the building. We remained still, listening as it came around toward the front door. I heard its familiar heavy breathing. I grabbed ahold of Jack, who helped me up. We moved away from the door. I said, "It's here."

Seconds later, it came bursting through the door, breaking it off its hinges. We all jumped away from it. Sheriff MacReedy came around with his rifle, grabbed me by my bad arm, and dragged me, shouting, "Come on, everybody, toward the holding cell!"

When we got there, he unlocked it. "Get in there and I'll lock it up! He shouldn't be able to break through this! Make sure you stay near the wall, so he doesn't reach you!"

"But, Sheriff…"

"Get in there now, missy before you get hurt!"

It looked like he was pointing his rifle at me. I glared at him. Then we heard a loud bang coming from the front room where his desk was. "Get in there now!" He left to go see what the noise was.

The guys were already in the cell, waiting for me to get in. Jack said, "Ash?" We heard another loud bang and a yell. I looked back at him. "Come on, baby! Get in here before that thing comes back here! Please!" I looked back toward where all the noise was coming from. He said, "Remember last night?"

I panned down to my ankle, but then I thought about all the other times I've seen it. I thought about earlier when we saw the three of them standing at the hilltop. I literally saw Roman, Kaden, and Glen standing there, just transformed into these beings. "It's them! It's got to be them!" I said to myself.

"What?"

I quickly shut the cell door, locked it, and took the keys out. The guys ran to me screaming, "What are you doing?" Jack grabbed ahold of my good arm. I yelled, "I have to go up there! I have to see if this creature is one of them!"

Jack begged me, "Please, Ashlynn, don't go! You

thought the same thing last night and look what happened."

"Yeah, but there's something different about this one! I can feel it!" I dropped the keys, grabbed his hand, and held it. "Please, baby! You trust me, right?"

"Of course, I do."

"Then let me go see. I promise I won't be long."

It took him a bit, but he squeezed my hand, and said, "Okay, but you better be back here soon."

I smiled. "Like I said last night, babe, you're stuck with me."

He smiled back and we kissed.

As I turned to take my first step, I said, "Well, this is going to be fun. Any advice on how to do this, doc?"

"Walk tenderly and try not to put any weight on it."

"Sound advice. Thanks."

Through the cell bars, Jack continued to hold onto my arm to help me steady myself. "Don't worry, I got you."

I took my first step and stumbled a little bit. Between the pain and the fact that I couldn't put too much pressure on it, I knew this wasn't going to be an easy trip. Thankfully, Jack still held on, otherwise I would've been on the floor. "Be careful, babe. Do you want me to help you?"

"No, I'm fine. I need to do this on my own. I just need to figure it out."

It took me a minute, but I began to limp back to the front of the station. Before going around the corner, I looked back at the guys. They were all watching me, concerned. Jack mouthed, "I love you."

I mouthed back, "I love you, too."

As I went around, I saw the sheriff was gone, but the creature stood. I looked at it. It looked at me.

"Hey."

It continued to stare at me. I thought about the three

creatures again. The creature that stood in front of me looked like the one who was smaller than the others. I recalled that Glen was the smallest of the group. I said, "Glen? Is…is that you?"

It was startled. It began to breathe heavily. Then, he gave me the peace sign. I had the same reaction he just had. I started to cry. I gave him the peace sign back. I then fell to the floor; my legs became so weak I just couldn't hold myself up anymore. He came right over to me to check on me. He went to wipe away the tears when I jumped a little from seeing this charred hand with long talon-like nails coming at me. I didn't mean to. It was kind of instinctive. He immediately pulled back his hand. I felt bad. I went to say something when he said, "It's okay. I jump too sometimes when I see what I look like now," in this hoarse voice.

I reached out, grabbed his hand, and placed it on my cheek. "Glen!"

He smiled.

I eyed him up and down, incredulous at what I was seeing. "Jesus! What the hell happened to you?"

He replied, "I was part of an experiment."

"Experiment?"

He nodded.

I couldn't help but start spitting out questions left and right, "What do you mean experiment? What happened? Where's Roman and Kaden?"

I was crying so hard I could barely breathe. That's when I felt him coming closer to me and wrapping his big, scaly arms around me. He was hugging me. I wrapped my arms around him tight. I didn't want to let go. As he held me, he said, "I'm sorry, Ashlynn."

I looked up at him. He looked down at me. We smiled at each other before I laid my head back down on his chest and we continued to hold each other. After a moment, when I was able to breathe and speak again, I asked him, "Was it you who stood outside the cabin?"

"Sometimes."

"And who attacked me yesterday?"

"It wasn't me."

I laughed and looked up at him. "Obviously."

He looked down at me. "I would *never* hurt you."

"I know…or Mom would kill you."

Even though it sounded like a growl, I knew he was chuckling at what I said. He continued, "It was…"

Then, he looked up and really growled. "What's wrong, Glen?"

I turned to see Sheriff MacReedy wielding his rifle with a little bit of blood trickling down the side of his head. "Get away from it, darlin'. It's dangerous and it needs to be killed."

"No, no, Sheriff. It's…" I went to stand up, but I couldn't with my bad elbow and bad ankle. Thankfully, Glen helped me up. I continued, "This is Glen, my brother. Remember?"

Angrily, he replied, "I know who it is! Now step aside, Ashlynn!"

I was floored. "Wh…What do you mean you know it's him?"

Smugly, he replied, "Who do you think recommended your boys to those scientists up the road?"

My heart dropped. "So that huge, white building near the cabin was a lab."

"Yeah, until these things destroyed it."

Glen continued to growl behind me. I asked, "Why?"

He replied, "They needed a couple of strong, young fellas who would be able to take some pain. I saw your brother and your friends as the perfect mice for their experiments.

And they gave me a pretty penny for them, too."

"You bastard! You took my family away from me!"

"Please, all I did was try and rid the world of three more delinquents. I've done it before, and I'll do it again."

"What the fuck is wrong with you?"

"Watch your mouth, young lady. And there's nothing wrong with me. I was bullied for most of my life, so I made a vow to protect the people from guys like them. I've done a pretty good job so far and I'm going to continue to do so."

"But my boys never did anything wrong!"

"Oh, really? Well, I looked them up. Roman is a party boy who has so many misdemeanors, I'm surprised he's not in jail. Kaden has priors from before he moved to New York and your brother," Glen growled at him, "he might have a clean record, but I guess you can say he was an innocent by-stander. I wasn't about to only take two in."

I wanted to vomit. "You're disgusting."

"No, I'm proactive. I did nothing wrong. They're the ones, however, terrorizing my town, scaring tourists, and de-stroying buildings."

I thought back to when I saw him outside the movie theater. "You knew. You knew when I saw you that day tak-ing pictures of the scratch marks that it could possibly be them and you didn't say anything. And you were 'so con-cerned', wanting to help me every single step of the way. I've cried on your shoulders numerous times, and you *never* said anything, you creep!" He looked down as if he was actually ashamed. "Did your cell phone even break, or did we really have the one second power outage?"

He looked me in the eyes, smirked, and shook his head. "But you believed every word I said."

I was seething. I limped over to him not feeling an ounce of pain. "I respected you! I…we saw you as a friend and what do you do? You use that friendship and betray us! You're the one who's the fucking monster!"

With his rifle, he pushed me down to the floor. "You need to relax, little lady, before I use this thing on you!"

Glen roared and charged at him. The sheriff shot off a round. He fell to the floor bleeding. I screamed, "No!"

I heard the guys screaming from the cell; yelling my name and threatening that if the sheriff hurts me, he's dead. However, I wasn't the one hurt. I crawled over to Glen. I picked up his head and held him in my arms. "Glen! Oh, god, hold on! You're going to be okay!"

He was breathing heavily. As I held him, I heard the rifle being cocked from behind me. I looked up and saw the sheriff pointing it right at me. "Get up, darlin'."

I looked back down at Glen.

"Now!" he hollered.

I slowly put his head down on the floor and stood up.

"Now, walk over to the holding cell."

As I limped over, I could see Jack and the others waiting to pounce on him. Jack snarled, "You harm her and I'll…"

"What? Attack me? From a locked cell? I would love to see you try. And if you *do* try anything once it's opened, she gets a bullet in her back, got it?" the sheriff commanded.

They immediately backed away from the door. He looked around for the keys. He found them, picked them up, and handed them to me. "Now, go ahead and unlock that door, darlin'." I stuck the key in the lock. "You know, y'all need to learn to mind your own damn business!"

That's when we heard more heavy footsteps coming from behind us. We turned to see two more creatures. I smiled, thinking I knew exactly who they were. *Roman! Kaden!*

Sheriff MacReedy pointed his rifle at them and shouted, "You bastards come in here and try to take over my town! I'll show you who's boss!"

I mustered up all the strength I had and kicked the rifle out of his hand with my good leg. It hurt like hell. I fell back into the cell door where I felt Jack's arms grab me. I grasped my bad ankle, wincing in pain. *Not exactly the smartest idea ever!*

Sheriff MacReedy turned to me, holding his wrist. He hollered, "What the hell do you think you're doing?!"

"What's right! Protecting my family!"

"You just made a big mistake, kicking a sheriff."

"No, it was you who made the mistake! Blood is thicker than water, asshole!"

That's when the two creatures came up from behind him, snatched him, and dragged him off. I pushed myself away from the cell, so they could unlock and open the door. Jack ran out and grabbed me, "Are you okay, hon?"

I nodded as I held him tight. "Yes, I'm alright." Then I remembered. "Glen!"

Jack helped me get over to him. He was still breathing heavily lying in a growing pool of his own blood. I fell beside him and held his head. "Glen hang on, please!"

Jerry sat beside me. "Here, Ash, let me take a look at him."

I moved out of his way. I told Glen, "He's a medic, bud. He's going to help you."

As Jerry examined him, I cried into Jack's arms. There were a couple of times Jerry must've pushed on a spot that really hurt because Glen roared, and Jerry jumped back. But instead of me calming him, Jerry did it. "I'm sorry, bud. I'm just trying to find where the bullet is."

After some time, Jerry said, "He's going to be okay." He looked up at me. "The bullet went into his side, here," pointing to the right side of Glen's torso, "but it looks like no major organs were hit. Just a lot of blood like with your ankle last night."

I smiled broadly as tears of joy streamed down my face. Jerry smiled back. "Once I clean him up and stitch him up, he's gonna be fine."

I let go of Jack, so I could squeeze Jerry. "Thank you, Jer!"

"No worries, girl." He let go of me. "Guys," pointing to Chad and Greg, "mind helping me pick him up and take him to the car?"

From behind us, we heard another gravelly voice say, "No need."

We all turned to see the other two creatures who just took out Sheriff MacReedy. I poked at Jack to help me up, which he did. I then limped over to them. "Kaden?" The one on the right nodded. I looked at the one on the left. "Roman!" He winked at me. *Oh, Roman, you flirtatious bastard!*

They walked over to me. I hugged them and held them tight. I cried. I couldn't believe I finally had my family back. Kaden grunted, "We're so sorry, Ashlynn."

I shook my head. "No, no don't apologize. I'm just glad I finally found you guys."

They then let go, so they could grab Glen. Roman stated, "Don't worry, guys. We'll take him back to the cabin." They went, picked him up, and carried him off while we got into Jack's rental to drive back and meet them. As Chad drove, Jack sat next to me, holding me. At one point, he asked, "You sure you're okay, hon?"

Grinning, I replied, "Yeah, I'm much better now."

****

When we got back to the cabin, Jerry went to work on Glen while I sat outside with Roman and Kaden by the lake. I kept on going back and forth on who I was leaning on, but it was mainly Kaden as it put less pressure on my ankle. It was throbbing, but I didn't care. I had my brothers back!

We stared at the lake, being comforted by the fact we were finally back together. At one point, I said out loud, "I should've tried harder." They looked at me. "When you guys left, I should've tried harder to stop you instead of letting you leave." I looked at them. "This is my fault."

Kaden exclaimed, "Don't you dare blame yourself for this, Ashlynn!"

Roman agreed, "This is not your fault at all."

"But if I tried harder to keep you guys here then this…"

Kaden interjected, "Ash, if we didn't leave, they would've harmed you."

"What?"

"They threatened to harm you if we didn't cooperate."

"Who?"

"Mainly, Sheriff MacReedy."

"That bastard!"

"However," Roman stressed, "we, along with others, destroyed the lab and got rid of the sheriff, making sure this wouldn't happen to anyone else."

I became concerned. "Wait, what do you mean others?"

Kaden stated, "There are more like us."

"More that escaped?"

"Yeah."

Roman clarified, "See, we were a part of these experiments that were supposed to change us into these like superhuman soldiers. It worked on some with no side effects, but then there were others, like us, that had some real bad side effects."

"This," I gestured to all of him, "is a real bad side effect?"

Kaden said, "Yeah. We should've been killed since we were 'mistakes', but we fought back."

"Did you guys kill anybody?"

"No. Not even the sheriff. We just told him that if he ever showed his face around here, we would make him look like us...our way," Kaden replied as he showed his razor-sharp claws.

Oh, thank God! I don't want my boys to become killers!

I waited a moment. "I have to ask. What type of experiments did they..."

Kaden interjected, "It's better if you don't..."

"But I wanna know."

He groaned and looked over at Roman who shrugged. "Dude, it's better to tell her now or else she'll haunt us until we do."

"Exactly."

With hesitation, he divulged, "Pretty much we were injected with some sort of serum every day. They were trying to splice our DNA with animal DNA to make us, like Roman said, 'superhuman.' Then we were tortured until there was some sort of result. If you became stronger or faster but stayed human, you passed. However, if you got stronger or faster and changed into," he motioned to himself, "this, you failed."

I was horrified. "Was this for the military?"

"Not military. Black Ops."

"Damn! But that means they could've been doing it for the military or for a government agency."

"Exactly."

"Why?"

Kaden was about to explain when Jerry came up from behind us. "Hey, guys," we turned our heads. As he wiped his hands with a towel, he explained, "It took some time, but I got the bullet out and stitched him up. He's sleeping right now, but he's gonna be fine."

My heart blossomed. "Thank you so much, doc for your help. How can I ever repay you?"

"My pleasure, Ash. Just keep on taking care of my boy."

We looked back to see Jack standing outside watching us from afar. I smiled and chuckled, "Oh, don't you worry. I'll be taking real good care of him once I'm better."

"That's too much information. I'm walking away now."

The boys and I laughed. Roman then looked over at Jack. He sneered, "So who's that guy anyway?"

"Jealous?"

"A little."

"That's Jack. I told you guys about him. He's the reason why I didn't date either of you. Well, at least you, Roman."

He growled at him.

"Oh, stop," I smacked him on his arm. "He's a good man."

Kaden asked, "Does he treat you well?"

"He's been treating me like a queen since day one, even way before we started dating."

Roman replied, "Then you have our blessings."

It meant the world to me that they, too, approved of Jack. Then Kaden inquired, "By the way, what's going on with you," gently touching my elbow and pointing to my ankle. "It looks like you're trying out for the lead in *The Mummy*."

"Well, the elbow was from when I first saw one of you and tripped over the rocking chair in the living room landing right on it." They both winced in pain. "Now I have a bruised elbow because of it, thank you very much," I looked at them.

They both said, "It wasn't me. It had to be Glen."

"Yeah, yeah, blame the youngest. And then my ankle was last night when I went out looking for you guys."

"Oh, and another by the way, what the hell were you thinking coming out here last night by yourself? You were extremely lucky it wasn't one of the bad ones who got you. You could've been killed before we found you," Roman ranted.

"I know. Jack kind of said the same thing when I told him my idea. I just thought that maybe if I came out by myself, you guys would've shown yourself instead of continuing to hide. I was figuring maybe seeing Jack and the others were scaring you away."

"Well…still…not exactly smart!"

I blurted out, "Wait, here's another by the way. This coming from a man who, when we went to Mexico, was okay with drinking their water because he said, and I quote, 'My stomach is made of steel. I'll be fine.' Then, after taking one sip, was puking his brains out and shitting himself so bad that he was in the hospital for at least a day. Do you really wanna fight about doing something stupid that could kill you?"

Kaden was dying. He rolled over onto his side, he was laughing so hard. Roman was about to retort when he realized I was right. "Touché."

Of course, Kaden had something to say, once he was able to breathe again, "I'm sorry, hon, but I have to agree with Roman. Thankfully, by the time we got to you, after we heard you screaming, you already took him out."

Roman rubbed my head like I was a little kid. "That's my girl."

"Hey, don't mess with the hair."

Kaden continued, "Seriously, though, Ash. If Cillian discovered you, you probably wouldn't be here right now, even if we tried to save you."

My heart dropped. My stomach tightened. "Holy shit,

you're serious."

"As a heart attack."

"So who's Cillian?"

"A bad dude that's at least twice our size and as strong as the three of us combined. That's all you need to know." And that's where we left it.

From there, I would come to find out that it was Kaden who carried me back to the camp last night. "I knew it was you," I said, beaming.

He smiled. "I took care of you while Glen and Roman took care of…" he looked at Roman, "did you guys figure out who that was?"

"Yeah, that scumbag, Nash."

My eyes widened. "Wait, Nash? You mean that asshole who groped me in the bar and you guys got into a fight with?"

Roman responded, "The very same."

"Shit. The last we saw of him he was being taken in by," here's that Mack truck again, "the sheriff!"

"And take a lucky guess where our buddy, the sheriff, sent him."

"The white building!"

"Bingo."

"Wow, it all comes full circle. And what do you mean you guys took care of him? You didn't kill him, right?"

Roman replied, "Nah, we just tied him to a tree and left him for dead."

"What?!"

"Jesus, Roman, don't give her a heart attack. Ash, he's fine. We were 'designed' to not need food, drink, or sleep for weeks on end. We can take punishment and heal rather quickly. We'll check in on him every so often."

"Maybe," Roman replied, harshly.

"Roman," Kaden barked.

I said, "Even though that bastard deserves it, I just don't want you guys to be killers. You would never hurt a fly. I'm just hoping those experiments didn't change you, mind wise."

"And they didn't," they both reassured me.

We talked some more before I asked Roman to go inside and check on Glen while Kaden and I stayed outside. I wanted some alone time with my best friend. I said to him, "It feels so good to have you back in my life."

He wrapped his arm around me and squeezed me against him. I continued, "But I do need answers, bud."

"And you deserve them, hon."

"And we both know if I asked these questions to Roman, I wouldn't get a straight answer." He nodded. "However, asking a man I trust just as much as I trust Jack is a totally different story. I mean we've always told each other everything. Shit, dude, you came out to me after asking me out on a date because that's how comfortable you were with me." He agreed. "But then everything changed when we came here. You know, my heart broke when you kept this secret from me. I thought we were losing our friendship."

He held me tighter. "I never want to lose the friendship we have. You are truly the greatest person in my life. But I hope you now understand why I did what I did. Why *we* did what we did."

I looked at him and nodded. "But I'm still utterly confused as to why you guys would agree to do something like this. You all are so smart. Why put yourself through this?"

He let out a long groan. As he unwrapped his arm from me to lay his arms on his knees, he said, "To make a long story short, the sheriff came to us saying there were some 'sports scientists' who wanted to try some stuff out on a couple of young guys like us. It was to help professional athletes."

"And you believed him?"

"No, not at first. Then he added that they would pay us handsomely if we did."

"Oh, shit! So Roman jumped at the opportunity."

"Exactly. You know how he is. Then when we saw it was in that building we stopped at, Glen and I immediately knew this wasn't going to be good. We tried to convince Roman to leave, but that's like trying to convince a kid to leave a playground." I smirked. It's so true, though. Roman's a good man with a good heart, but sometimes I would love to strangle him or bang his head against the wall. He can do such stupid things. Kaden continued, "When we walked in, the sheriff was there, which I thought was weird. Then they made us sign a bunch of forms, swearing us to secrecy, making us agree to come back every day no matter what. That's when the sheriff said that if we didn't follow through, he would hurt you."

I shook my head. "That son of a bitch. When did this happen?"

"One of the last times we were at the bar with him."

"Where the hell was I?"

"The bathroom, I think."

I recalled, "Oh, that was the night I walked back and Roman was all giddy while you and Glen looked like you were about to murder him."

"Yup. The sheriff warned us then not to tell you because he didn't want you to get involved. He kept on saying it was a 'guy' thing."

With each passing sentence Kaden said, my fury grew, but, at the same time, I was so relieved. I had my family back. The sheriff was gone. There was literally nothing more

I could ask for.

****

Kaden and I continued to talk as the sun began to set. I asked him about the other creatures that were like him. He told me that some came out worse than them: barely able to speak, their skin worse than theirs, and their dispositions meaner. I quivered at the very thought that there were legit monsters – including Nash and whoever this Cillian was – out in the woods that I've called my second home for so long.

After a while, I decided to go inside to see how Glen was doing. Kaden helped me hobble in. Glen sat up as we walked in, the right side of his torso heavily taped up, while Roman was looking out the window. I said to him, "Seriously, dude, jealousy is a bad look on you."

"Remember, I saw you first."

I laughed. "Yeah, yeah." I went over to Glen, "Hey, bro! How you doing?"

"Better knowing you're okay. You?"

"Same." I smiled from ear to ear. I went and sat next to him on the table. "If Mom ever finds out we put our butts on this table, she'll kill us."

Glen laughed. "Or that surgery was performed on it." "Yeah, that too."

I laid my head on his arm and held his hand. Kaden and Roman stood by the glass doors in the dining room, watching the sky turn darker and darker. I jested, "What are you guys waiting for, an army to come find you?"

They turned and glared at me. My smile vanished. I picked up my head. "Holy shit, you guys are watching out for something."

Kaden responded, "Like I told you, hon there are others out there like us who aren't as nice. And with the sheriff loose, he might get some reinforcements and come back."

I recalled. "The gunshots and the roars that we heard earlier, was that?"

They nodded.

From behind us, we heard, "Who did this to you guys?" It was Chad calling from the living room.

Kaden responded, "The Black Ops."

"Wow. Well, by now they probably moved on to a different town, which is worse."

"True, but after earlier today we don't know for sure, so we're going to have to keep our guard up."

Chad agreed. Then we heard in the background, "Dude, give them some privacy. They haven't seen each other in months."

"Yeah, yeah. Jack being right."

"As always," I remarked.

"Damn right," he yelled back. We all laughed.

After a moment, I suggested, "Why don't you guys come back with us then? Get away from here?"

"We've made the forest our home, Ash. We'll be able to hide in it," Glen said.

"But I would be more comfortable if you left with me. At least I could protect you and make sure you're safe."

Kaden said, "Hon, we love you, but we couldn't ask you to risk your life for ours."

"I'm not asking…"

"Well, then I'm telling you."

I flipped my hair at him. "Fine."

He laughed.

As we played catch-up, I continued to feel a throbbing pain in my ankle. Glen rubbed my back as I winced in pain. "You okay?"

"This certainly doesn't tickle."

Kaden said, "We're sorry, hon. We didn't know until we heard you screaming."

"And I'm going to get mad at you guys for not always protecting me. Please."

"Well, that's why we made camp not too far away from here. Remember how I said we would be watching over you?" I nodded. "Well, when we escaped and destroyed the lab, we immediately thought of you, of course. We hoped you might've gone home, but when we saw you were still here, we watched over you. We wanted to make sure you were safe; that the sheriff didn't go after you or that the others didn't find you. Unfortunately, a couple of them did eventually find you. One of them got really close the one night."

"Yeah, I remember. I unfortunately won't ever forget that night."

Glen said, "We stopped him before he figured a way in."

"So the loud screams I heard were you guys attacking him?"

They all nodded. "Again, we didn't kill him. We just made sure he understood not to come into the area," Kaden reaffirmed.

I had to verify. "Please tell me I've been seeing you guys outside the cabin or in the woods...up until last night, obviously."

Kaden replied, "Yes. Every single time."

"Oh, thank God! So, who did I see first?"

Glen slightly raised his hand. "That was me and it was...well...by accident."

I gaped at him. "By accident?"

He added, "Yeah, I was sticking my head out a little too far. We never wanted you to see us like this, but I guess it was going to happen no matter what."

"So, wait a minute, it was you who scared the crap out of me from the very beginning?"

He smiled.

I slightly pushed him. "You little shit. You're the reason why I have a bruised elbow."

We all laughed. He said, "And I watched you fall. I felt so bad, but at the same time I was laughing so hard. I was the one who left you the note."

We continued to talk, laugh, and have fun. It was like we picked up from where it all stopped, like nothing ever happened. Like nothing ever changed. After some time, Jack came into the dining room. "Hey, baby."

I turned to him. "Hey, babe." He looked nervous. I asked, "You okay, Jack? Don't forget, it's Glen and my friends. They're not going to hurt you."

"Well, I might," Roman joked. At least I hope he was joking.

Glen, Kaden, and I yelled, "Shut up, Roman!"

"What? He stole my girl."

"God, you're unbelievable. Just ignore him, babe."

Glen decided to be cute. He waved at him. "Hey, Jack."

Jack smiled. "Hi, Glen. Uh, no, it's not that. I'm more afraid of how you're going to respond to what I'm about to say."

"Okay." I was a little fearful.

"I think we should really leave here tomorrow morning. If what they're saying is true, then it's not safe and we need to get out of here like right now. Ideally, I would like to leave tonight, but there's no more flights leaving the airport back to California."

I silently breathed out but also became annoyed. I was about to respond when Kaden said, "I agree."

I peered over at him. My annoyance became shock. I

said, "No, I'm not leaving you guys. I finally found you after months of searching. I don't care if the sheriff comes back with an army."

Glen exclaimed, "I do!"

Kaden and Roman said, in unison, "Me too!"

Even though they were right, I still didn't like the idea of leaving them. "Please don't let me lose you guys again."

Kaden and Roman walked over to me. Glen opened his arms wide, and I fell into him. Kaden, caressing my good arm, said, "You'll never lose us. We will always be here for you."

Eventually, Glen, Roman, and Kaden left to watch over the cabin while I tried to get some rest. They promised to be back in the morning to say their goodbyes.

OCTOBER 3rd

My boys did not disappoint.

While sitting on the counter in the kitchen to let Jerry clean up my ankle and re-wrap it, I saw them coming out of the woods. I waved at them like a child who sees their parents after coming out of school. They waved back. Jerry said, "Things are looking good, Ash. How does it feel?"

"Better than yesterday. At least it's not throbbing as bad, but it sucks that I can't really walk on it."

"Yeah, but that won't be forever. What about your elbow?"

"Eh. I'm able to move it," as I showed him.

"Good. And the scratches on your face are looking better, as well. Before we head over to the airport, we'll stop at Dr. Park's office to get everything checked out for you."

"Is that why we're catching like a 2 pm flight?"

"Yup. I made sure of that."

"Best doc ever."

"Do you remember the story we came up with?" Jerry inquired.

"Yup, hopefully he believes it."

"Yeah, hopefully."

I waited a moment before saying, "Jer, I seriously cannot thank you enough for not only helping me but for saving my brother's life. It truly means the world to me. How can I repay you for everything you did?"

"It was my pleasure, Ash. Like I said, just take care of my boy, but please don't repeat what you said last night. I don't need those images in my head."

We both laughed. "Okay, I won't." I looked over to see Jack standing in the living room packing things up. "But we've been there for each other for over twenty years. I plan on being there for him for another twenty more and beyond."

Jerry grinned. "Perfect answer."

Once we packed everything into the car – which the boys kindly helped us do – and made sure we had all of our belongings, I gave Roman a hug first. He tried to grab my butt like he always did, but instead of smacking his hand away, I just let him grab it. "This is the only time I will let you grab my ass."

"Oh, come on, babe. I've been through a lot."

"Okay, maybe one more time," I laughed. "I'm just glad you didn't lose that charming personality of yours."

I gave him a kiss on the cheek. I then went to Kaden. I gave him a hug. "Thank you for everything, Kaden. I'm going to miss our talks and your philosophical babble."

He laughed. "It's not babble."

I squeezed him. "I love you so much."

"I love you, too, Ash."

"Oh, and I have a gift for you," I let go of him and reached into my jean pocket, "well, I guess you can say I'm regifting it." I pulled out his shirt and handed it to him.

He grabbed it. "I thought you wanted it."

I looked at him. "How did you know?"

"Because that guy was out here searching for it saying, 'I need to find that shirt or Ashlynn is going to be so upset.'"

I laughed out loud. "Then it must've been you who scared him."

He shrugged.

"Poor, Mr. Scarlo. Well, I did want it if I never found you guys, but since you're standing right in front of me, I figured I would give it back to you. Use it as a way for me to identify you guys when I come back."

"You got it, hon."

Finally, I went to Glen. I wrapped my arms tight around him. I didn't want to let go of my baby brother. I said to him, "I don't want to leave you, Glen. I promised that I would always protect you."

"And you did. Now go and take care of yourself. I'll be fine." I continued to hold him. "Be happy with Jack."

As I held onto him, I felt more arms wrap around me. I looked up to see Roman and Kaden joining in the "hug fest". Then I heard Jack clear his throat. I let go and turned toward him. He said, "I'm sorry, babe, but we need to get going. You have a doctor's appointment to get to and a flight to catch."

"Okay."

I gave each of them one last hug and kiss on the cheek before getting into Jack's rental. As we drove off, I looked back to see my boys one last time. They were already up the hill watching us leave.

"Goodbye, my loves. Be safe."

****

As we walked into his office, Dr. Park greeted us, "Hi again, Ashlynn." Then he saw me being, pretty much, carried in and the scratches on my face."

"Oh my goodness, what happened?"

"I stepped onto a bear trap."

He winced in pain. "Geez, how in the world did you do that? Did you not see it?"

I looked at Jack and Jerry, who brought me in. "Nope, it was so well hidden, I couldn't even tell."

"And that caused the scratches on your face?"

"Oh, that's from when I fell after it closed on me. I went face first."

"Excuse my language, but damn!"

We laughed. "Yeah, I know."

"Do you know who put that out?"

"I have family taking care of it," I replied, smirking at Jack and Jerry.

"Good. I hope when you do find out that you sue them. They must be new to the area and don't know the animal control laws around here."

I shrugged. "I guess."

"Alright, well, let's get you to the X-ray room and see what's going on."

After examining my ankle and the results from the X-ray, he determined, "Thankfully, Ashlynn, like Jerry first diagnosed, you don't have a compound fracture, but you do have multiple non-displaced fractures in your ankle and foot." He showed us on the X-ray where they were. "For now, I'm going to put you in a boot because I want you to get a CT scan and make sure there's not more or anything deeper than those fractures. After you get that done, though, as long as it's not worse than it seems, I want you in a cast. Are you still staying here?"

"No, we're actually catching a flight in a little while to head home."

"Okay, once you're home, I want you to see a foot doctor and get that CT scan. Again, I can only do so much in my little office."

"Yeah, I know. Thank you so much, Dr. Park for your help."

"My pleasure. Now, Ashlynn," he once again leaned against the counter. *Oh, crap! What now?* "You said you got caught in a bear trap, correct?"

"Yup," I replied, trying to sound as convincing as possible.

"Are you sure? Because anybody who gets caught in a bear trap 99.9% of the time lose their limbs. The metal jaw goes right into the bone. With you, everything is still intact, you just have the small fractures and scraps on your skin. Some deeper than others. It looks like you were mauled by something instead of being stuck in the trap. Are you telling me the truth?"

My heart leapt into my throat. He noticed. "Please, don't be frightened, Ashlynn. It's not like I'm going to tell the authorities or anything. Remember, I do have the Hippocratic Oath to abide by."

I looked at Jack with eyes screaming, "Help me!"

He stepped up and said, "Well, Dr. Park, you did say that '99.9% of the time, people lose their limbs.' Fortunately, Ashlynn is in that extremely small percentile that didn't have to lose her foot, or it wasn't that badly damaged. She's very lucky."

Not believing a word he said, Dr. Park replied, "Yes, very." He then switched his attention over to Jerry. "Now, Jerry, you're the one who's been taking care of this, correct?"

"Yes, sir."

"You did a great job. How come you didn't pursue a career in the medical field?"

"Well, I did for a little while, but realized my true passion was in filming, so now I'm a cameraman."

"Oh, really? What do you film?"

"Well, I've been…"

I interrupted him, "Sorry, Dr. Park, not to be rude, but we do have a flight to catch."

He smiled. "You're right. I'm sorry. Let me go get that boot for you." Once he finished booting my ankle, he said, "Okay, Ashlynn you're all set. I just want to double-check your elbow."

"Sure."

After examining it, he said, "Alright, Ashlynn it looks like you're good. Here's the referral for the CT scan. Please get that done once you're home."

I took the referral from him. "I will. Thanks, Dr. Park."

Then we heard a growl coming from outside. It was similar to the growls of the creatures. I jumped and looked at Jack and Jerry who looked at me.

Dr. Park said, "There's that sound again. It's so odd. I never heard anything like it."

Oh, no!

"You mean you've heard this sound before, Dr. Park?" Jack questioned.

"Yes, I've been hearing it for a couple of weeks now. Not every day, but every so often. I would go outside to see what it is and here this thunderous noise like heavy footsteps running away. I guess it's true, Bigfoot is in the area."

Dr. Park laughed while we did more of a nervous laugh. I thought, *Shit, that's got to be one of the monsters! There's no way that could be Glen or Roman or Kaden! I know they can be fast, but I don't think they're that fast!*

As we were preparing to leave, Jack texted Chad to make sure "the coast was clear." When he responded, "Yes," we rushed out to the car and headed for the airport.

DECEMBER 23rd

For the past couple of months, I have been living with Jack as I waited for my ankle to heal. He has been taking amazing care of me: taking me to get the CT scan done (which we did about a day or two after landing to find nothing else was wrong), taking me to my doctors appointments, cooking for me…he pretty much has done anything and everything for me. He has truly been the best boyfriend in the world.

A couple of days after we landed, I decided I wasn't going back to New York and to *Replay*. It wasn't exactly the easiest decision for me to make but with the boys "gone", there was nothing there for me. Even Jack agreed. When I called Mr. Schneider to tell him, I first told him that I found the boys and they were okay. He was ecstatic. He even cried. He always looked at all his workers as his children – except for any that were around his age, then they were more like brothers or sisters. But when I told him none of us were coming back, he wasn't exactly thrilled. "I just lost four of my best people to this damn vacation!" he exclaimed.

I apologized profusely. It took him some time, but he composed himself and wished me the best of luck. Before hanging up, he said, "You know, and I'm saying this truthfully from my heart, you were my favorite employee and I have always looked at you as my daughter. You did amazing things here at *Replay* and I know you're going to do amazing things wherever you end up. Please call me if you ever need anything. I am always here for you."

Once I hung up the phone, I said to Jack, who was sitting next to me on the couch, "Well, that's that," as I wiped away tears. "That's definitely on my top 10 list of hardest conversations I've ever had in my life."

"Wait until you tell your parents about the guys."

"Ha. That'll become number one the second I start that conversation."

"You did the right thing, though, by leaving."

"I know," I said with a heavy heart. "I just…I loved that job. It was truly the best job I ever had. And Mr. Schneider was such a sweetheart to all of us." I continued to use the tissue Jack gave me to wipe away more tears.

Jack asked, "So now what?"

"I honestly have no clue," I replied, shrugging.

"Did you have any ideas in mind?"

"Not really," I said as I leaned into him, and he wrapped his arm around me. "I mean, I was thinking about maybe moving back in with my parents and seeing about finding a job in Florida, but…" I looked at him. "You have something up your sleeve, don't you?"

He smiled. "Well, I do have an idea."

"Oh. Do tell."

"Stay here with me."

I beamed. I quivered with excitement but tried to hide it. "And what would I do?"

"Work with me. Be my assistant or my researcher or whatever you want to be."

"You've thought about this, haven't you?!"

"A little," he said with that innocent and handsome

smile of his.

"And you don't think we're moving too quickly?" I asked with sincerity. I mean, a lot of people would think this.

"If we met yesterday, yeah absolutely. But we've known each other for so many years, Ash. I think we would be kidding ourselves if we both didn't dream of this moment, so why not take this next step?"

He's right!

My cheeks might've been stinging in pain, but I couldn't stop smiling. "Alright, then! Let's do it!"

He hooted and hollered, and we kissed. That night became the greatest night of my life…well, one of them.

****

A couple of weeks ago, since my ankle was finally out of the cast, we went to New York to grab my stuff. Fortunately, I had clothes from the vacation that I was able to wear; however, nothing was exactly winter-friendly. It got pretty cold in Sacramento. Jack offered to buy me new clothes, but when I already have all the clothes I need – they were just in a different state – I declined his sweet offer. Although, we did go out to grab a couple of things to last me until we made the move.

Upon walking into the apartment, I was reminded very quickly that I wasn't the only one who lived in it. Glen's stuff was there as well. It was bittersweet for me seeing all of his stuff. Jack asked, "What do you want to do with it, babe?"

"Can we pack it up and bring it with us? I just can't bear to part with it right now."

"Of course."

As we went through my stuff, packing whatever I was keeping and trashing whatever I wasn't, I constantly found photos of me with the boys. They were all over the apartment except for one place. Jack got a little upset. "Why aren't there any pictures of us around?"

"Check my bedroom on the nightstand," I replied. He looked. "Aw, there I am."

Scanning through the photos of me with Glen, Roman, and Kaden made my heart dance knowing they were okay. They were alive. Even though they look very different now, I didn't care. As long as they were still here, it didn't matter to me what they looked like.

While in New York, I also visited *Replay*. It was so nice to see Mr. Schneider and the crew. He came up to me and gave me a huge hug. I also introduced him to Jack. "Oh, so this is the young man you've been dreaming of for some time."

I blushed. "Yes." Even Jack blushed a little.

Now, here we are. Fully moved in, living together, and loving every second of it.

Today, though, we left to go spend Christmas in the warmth of Florida with my parents. I haven't seen them since they left to go take care of my grandmother. They know that Jack and I are living together and are actually okay with it. However, as of right now, they think the boys stayed in Washington because Glen and Roman met some girls and Kaden met a guy. They don't even know about my attack yet, so if they see me limping, that's going to be a fun conversation. I'm fine until I've either stood on it too long or walked on it too much; that's when it starts to bother me. *I guess we'll see.*

Once we arrived in Florida, I asked Jack, "You have the tape, right?"

"Yes, hon. That's like the one-hundredth time you asked me."

"I mean, should we even tell them? Do you think they'll believe us even with the tape?"

"Babe, you need to tell your parents the truth. Whether they believe us or not is a hurdle we'll jump through once we get there."

"Together?"

He gently squeezed my hand. "Together."

My parents were right at the gate as we walked out. My mom was waving her arms around, jumping up and down like she was at a freaking concert. *Oh god!*

She ran over to me yelling, "My baby's home!"

She grabbed me and held me like she hadn't seen me in years. I said to her, "Mom, I love you and I'm so happy to see you too, but you're making a scene."

"Oh, stop it! I'm your mother, I'm allowed!"

As we held each other, my dad went over to Jack with his hand held out. "Jack."

He shook his hand. "Dad."

"Thank you for taking care of and protecting my little girl."

"My pleasure, sir."

I let go of my mom and went to my dad. "Hi, Daddy!"

"Hi, princess," he said with a huge smile on his face and tears welling up in his eyes. We gave each other a tight hug. "I'm so happy to see you safe."

"Me too, Daddy."

We gathered up our luggage and headed to the car. I started limping a little after we stood around waiting for our bags and catching up. Plus, they parked pretty far. Even though my limp was slight, my dad saw it. "Ashlynn, how come you're limping? What happened?"

CRAP! "Uh…because…I got it caught in a bear trap," I replied, unconvincingly, almost questioning myself.

"A bear trap?!" both of my parents shouted, stopping mid-stride.

"Yeah."

I looked up at Jack who looked at me. His eyes said it all, "Really? You went with that?"

My mom then started in. "What do you mean a bear trap? How did you step in a bear trap? Where was it? Were you by Ned's yard because you know how paranoid he can be? Which, by the way, I spoke to him…"

Good lord make it STOP!

"Hey, Mom," Jack said. "Not to be disrespectful, but I know Ashlynn is hungry. We didn't eat anything on the plane ride because it didn't look too good. Can we eat first and ask questions later? I mean as you can see Ashlynn is fine. She starts to limp a little bit after standing on it or walking on it too much, but I know she would feel so much better with food in her stomach."

We all stood in silence for a minute. If there's one thing you do not do in life, it's stopping a panicky Italian mother in the middle of her rant. Then my dad said, "You're absolutely right, Jack. I'm famished myself. We have dinner waiting for you guys at home, so let's go."

Thank you, God!

"But that doesn't mean you're in the clearing, young lady. You have *a lot* of explaining to do."

My parents walked away. Jack looked at me and whispered, "Well, it worked for a second."

After eating dinner and cleaning up, we all went into the living room to sit down and talk. My dad said, "Alright, now tell us what happened to your ankle, Ashlynn."

I took in a deep breath. "Okay, so," I looked over at Jack who nodded. "Jack and I have something to show you."

My mom immediately exclaimed, "Oh my gosh, you're pregnant!"

"What? No, Mom!"

"Oh," she replied, disappointed.

Jesus, Ma! "No, we have a video we want to show you that will kind of explain everything: my ankle, what happened to the boys…"

My mom interjected, "What do you mean what happened to the boys? I thought you said they all found someone to be with." She thought for a second and gasped. "Oh my gosh, are you going to show us a sex video?"

"Oh my god, Mom!" I rubbed my forehead so hard it was like I was digging a hole into it.

"For Pete's sake, Nancy, Ashlynn would never show us that."

"Well, she said the video will explain what happened to the boys, so I thought…"

I became irritated. "Look, I've been lying to you guys," I finally spat out.

"What?" they said, unanimously. I think what scared me the most when they said it was how their voices pierced me and made my bones tremble. I've never really lied to them before, admittingly anyway. When I broke about the boys missing, that was different. Now, I'm legitimately telling them I lied. It was a mixture of disappointment, anger, and sadness.

Here we go! "I'm sorry, but I've been lying to you guys about the boys, and I lied about the bear trap."

"Why would you do such a thing, Ashlynn? We didn't raise you to lie, especially to your parents," my mom said.

"Because I was afraid you wouldn't believe me. That's why Jack and I have this video to share with you. This shows the truth."

Both of my parents calmed down a little. My dad replied, "Princess, no matter how ludicrous your story may sound, we'll believe you. We love you, never forget that."

"I know and I'm sorry, Dad, but when I called and told Mom the first time about what I saw, she didn't believe me. I thought if I continued, you guys would've thought I was insane."

My mom retorted, "Well, you were talking about seeing monsters outside the cabin."

Jack stepped in. "She wasn't lying about that, Mom. My crew and I saw it as well and we have the evidence to prove it."

"Then let's see it," my dad said.

Without any hesitation, Jack shot up and got the DVD rolling. As they watched it, my parents' mouths were wide open and their eyes were so far out of their heads, I thought they were going to pop out. My mom asked, "So that's what you saw when you called me?"

I nodded. "And then there was one night I went out to search for it on my own…"

"You went out all by yourself?! Jack, why didn't you go with her or stop her?!" my dad roared.

Before Jack could defend himself, I said, "We will get to that in a minute, Dad, but when I did, one of them attacked me and dragged me through the forest. That's why my ankle is a little messed up."

"One of them? You mean there's more than one?" my mom yelled out.

My dad bellowed, "That's it! I'm selling the cabin!"

Jack and I looked at each other. He said, "No, Dad. You don't want to do that quite yet."

"And why not?"

It took me a minute, but I finally explained, "That creature in the video could either be Glen or Roman or Kaden. Or it could be somebody else I can't really tell, but...your boys now look like that creature."

They stared at us. Tears rolled down my mother's cheeks. She questioned, "How?"

I told them everything. My mom continued to cry. My dad wrapped his arm around her and rubbed her shoulder. I began to cry, too. Jack rubbed my back and held me. Once I finished, my dad fumed, "I knew there was something I didn't like about that sheriff. And you, young lady," I looked up at him, "going out there all by yourself. That was so foolish! You could've been killed!"

"I know, but I just needed to find out on my own if what I thought was true. And I was right, I just didn't know there were others out there who saw me more as their next meal."

After a moment of silence, my mom shocked us all by saying, "I want to go see them."

My dad, Jack, and I just stared at her in disbelief. She continued, "Glen is still my baby boy. And Roman and Kaden are still my boys, too. I don't care if they are these...creatures. I refuse to call them monsters because they are not monsters." I agreed. "Whether any of you like it or not, I want to go see them."

Jack responded, "As well as you should, Mom. If we ever go back for the show, you are more than welcome to join us."

"Why not now?" she became defensive.

"I don't think right now is safe, especially if anybody is there searching for them. We should really wait for things to settle down first."

"You mean, someone is after my boys?"

"We're not a hundred percent sure, but it's possible," Jack replied.

My mom was so distraught. This was not how I wanted to spend Christmas with my parents. I had no clue what to do or say to make her feel better about this.

While my parents stayed downstairs to talk, Jack and I went up to our room. I sat on the bed and said, "Well, that went well."

"Yeah. Your mom surprised me when she said she wanted to go see them."

"I actually wasn't too surprised by that."

"Really?"

"Yeah, I actually can't believe she didn't plow right through us to get in the car and start driving there herself."

Jack chuckled. "That's true."

"I just feel so helpless right now. I mean all she wants to do is see her sons and we're denying her that. How messed up is that?"

"Baby, that's not your fault. That's nobody's fault. We're just playing it safe."

"I know. It still sucks, though."

He sat next to me, rubbing my back. As I fell deeper and deeper under his spell, my eyes closed. I could've fallen asleep just like that. But then he stopped and got up. I whined, "No, don't stop. That was feeling really good."

He said, "I'll continue rubbing your back for the rest of my life if you say 'Yes.'"

I opened my eyes, puzzled at what he said. Then I saw him in front of me, on one knee, with a beautiful square-shaped diamond ring sitting in its box. My eyes widened. "I was going to save this for tomorrow, but I think right now is a better time." I cupped my hands over my mouth. "Ashlynn Angela Amuso, will you be my wife?"

I shouted, "Yes, yes, a thousand times yes!"

He jumped up. "Yes!" He took the ring out of the box and put it on my finger. We kissed and hugged each other. "I love you so much, Ashlynn."

"I love you, too, Jack."

Seconds later we heard my parents running up the stairs. "Is everything okay?"

They came to the door. I declared, "Jack and I are getting married!"

My parents were overjoyed. My dad took out the "good" champagne to toast to our new journey. It was good to be happy and celebrating life instead of being depressed about something we had no control over.

OCTOBER 3rd

Today has become the fifth greatest day of my life – well in recent memory. First, it was Jack and I finally starting our relationship. Second was finding the boys, third was Jack and I deciding to live together, fourth was Jack proposing, and now, today, Jack and I are officially husband and wife. The best part, we went back to Lake Minnetaha, so the boys could be a part of it.

When Jack and I first started planning the wedding, nothing seemed right. Every place we looked at, every place we thought of just didn't fit. It felt empty. It felt like something was missing. One night, Jack asked me, "What's wrong, babe? Why is nothing feeling right to you?"

I immediately responded, "Because Glen won't be there. And Roman and Kaden. It just wouldn't be right to me to get married without my brothers by my side."

Jack's response made me fall in love with him even more. "Then why don't we get married in Lake Minnetaha?"

I blossomed. "Really babe?! You would be okay with that?!"

"Absolutely!"

I became so elated, but realized, "Wait, we can't have all of our guests there. Everybody would react horribly to them and call the police or something."

"Who said we invite everybody to this celebration? Or even anybody?"

I looked at him with bright eyes. "Are you saying what I think you're saying?"

"Have an extremely small ceremony there and then if you want to have a bigger celebration with family and friends here, then we'll do that."

I hugged him so tight I think he stopped breathing for a second. "Just when I thought I couldn't love you anymore, you prove me wrong. I love this idea! Thank you so much, baby!" Then it hit me, "But wait," I still held onto him with my arms outstretched so I could look at him, "who would marry us?"

"Chad. He's an ordained minister."

I laughed. "Of course, he is." I continued to hug him. "There is one major thing I need there, though."

"What's that, babe?"

I let go of him. "My parents. I don't think they'll ever forgive us if we got married without them or if we went to Lake Minnetaha and didn't bring them."

"Well, duh."

So, it was settled. It'll be Jack, myself, my parents, Chad (our minister), Jerry (our videographer), and Greg (our extra man in the group) traveling to Lake Minnetaha so my boys could see me get married. When I told my parents, they *loved* the idea. We decided to do it around our one-year anniversary, which gave us time to find rings, a dress, etc.

"This couldn't be any more perfect!"

****

Yesterday, my parents met up with us in Sacramento, so we could travel all together. As we began driving toward the cabin from the airport, I could see my parents had mixed emotions running through them. They were anxious. They were excited. They were scared.

When we pulled up to the cabin, I said to them, "Why don't you guys get settled in while Jack and I go find the boys."

My dad said, "What if there's another one of those monsters out there that's not them?"

Jerry asked, "Would you guys be opposed to me joining you? I'll tape the reunion, plus there'll be a third person in the group just in case of anything."

I replied, "I'm cool with that. Feel better, Dad?"

"A little bit. But if anything happens you scream, you got it. I'll do my best to save you."

"I will, Daddy." I gave my mom and dad a hug and kiss on the cheek before heading out.

Jerry, Jack, and I walked up the hill where we believed their "home" was. Jerry asked, "How do you know they're there for sure?"

I shook my head. "I don't, I'm just hoping they are."

We walked up to the edge, looked around, and to our right saw three creatures lying on the ground relaxing. I knew it was them because Kaden was "wearing" the shirt I regifted him before we left. Well, it was more like he draped it on top of himself. I highly doubt it'll fit him anymore. *I knew he would listen!*

My heart soared. Ecstatic is not even the word to describe how happy I was to see them. It was more than that. I remembered our group motto and yelled out, "All for one…"

They looked up and replied, "Fuck you, I ain't sharing!"

They immediately got up and ran toward us as I ran toward them. We met about halfway in a huge group hug.

Then I went around giving hugs and kisses to each. I went to Roman last because I knew he would try to grab my butt and he did, which was perfect. I swatted at his hand. "Nope. No more of that, my friend."

"Aw, come on, babe. I've been through a lot."

"Dude, you used that line a year ago. It's not going to work now. But there's another reason why you can't."

"What's that?"

I showed my left hand. "We're getting married!"

We all jumped up and down like teenage girls. They went to Jack and gave him a hug. Glen said, "It's about damn time I get to call you my brother-in-law."

Roman asked, "So did you guys come all the way out here just to tell us that?"

"No, you ass. We're here so you guys can be a part of the ceremony."

Kaden said, "Aw, sweetie. But wait…who else is here then? Is it anybody who would…"

"No, don't worry. The other people here would never say a word."

Relieved, he replied, "Oh, good. So then who is it?"

"Chad and Greg, the other guys on Jack's team, and…Mom and Dad."

They became upset. Glen said, "Ashlynn, Mom and Dad can't see us like this. They'll lose their minds."

"They already know."

Kaden inquired, "What do you mean they already know?"

"Last year, at Christmas, I showed them a video of a creature walking past one of the cameras we had out here and told them that's what you guys look like now. Afterwards, they wanted to come out and see you guys. Mom insisted."

Glen said, "I don't know if I could face her like this."

I rubbed his shoulder. "You gonna have to, little bro."

After some time, they worked up the courage to come back with us to the cabin. While we walked, I asked, "So did anybody come looking for you guys after we left?"

Kaden replied, "Yes, but we hid well enough that they left thinking we were either dead or somewhere else."

I breathed a sigh of relief. "Oh, thank, God."

As we came up to the cabin, I said, "Do you guys want to come inside, or do you want me to bring them out here?"

It took a moment, but Kaden answered, "Bring them out here. I just feel like it'll be better if they saw us outside than in the cabin."

I nodded. "Okay, then I'll be right back."

I went inside and grabbed my parents. "Are you guys ready?"

They both took in a deep breath and nodded. We went outside toward the backyard where we set up camp a year ago. My dad held my mom as they followed me. As they saw them, my mom gasped, but I don't think it was out of fear. It was more out of shock; she couldn't believe she was finally seeing them again. They slowly walked over. My mom let go of my father and was heading straight for Glen.

Oh my gosh, she recognizes him! I put my hand over my mouth and began to cry. I fell into Jack as I was about to fall to my knees. She walked right up to him, looked him straight in the eyes, and said, "Glenny?"

"How did you know, Mom?"

Tears streamed down her cheeks. "I'll never forget my

baby boy's eyes," and embraced him.

You couldn't tell but the boys were crying, too. My dad went up to Glen and hugged him. "It's good to see you again, son."

After some time, my mom let go of Glen and walked over to Roman and Kaden. She wiped away her tears and said, "Wait, don't tell me. I want to figure out who's who on my own."

The guys stood there with smiles on their faces. She stared at their eyes for a little while until she finally said, "You're Roman," pointing at Roman, "and you're Kaden," pointing at Kaden. I was dumbfounded. I couldn't believe she figured them out so easily. Kaden asked, "How did you know, Mrs. Amuso?"

"Because you always had the look of innocence in your eyes while this one was always more mischievous." Roman shrugged. "And what did I tell you about that 'Mrs. Amuso' crap, come over here and give your mom a hug."

With no hesitation, they jumped right into her arms. We spent the rest of the day eating (shocker), catching up, laughing, crying…you know, all the fun stuff that happens at reunions.

Then this afternoon I said "I do" to a man I was ready to marry years ago with my brothers by my side. It was stunning and it was perfect. It was more than I could've ever imagined.

Greg, Jerry, and Chad built an arch from branches, sticking leaves and flowers throughout the top of it. They placed it at the edge of the forest in the backyard. They ran a white aisle runner from the cabin to the arch, laying purple rose petals along the way. Jerry took photos of my dress, my flowers, our rings, and of me getting ready. I said to him, "Dude, are you like a jack of all trades?"

He laughed. "Pretty much. Except I can't cook or bake."

Jack and I got ready in separate rooms. You know, the whole "it's bad luck to see the bride before the wedding" myth. I may not be a traditionalist, but there was one thing I wanted: to see Jack's face as I walked down the aisle and that look was priceless. As I had my dad to my right and Glen to my left, I walked down just gazing at him. My favorite feeling came back. For that moment, everybody and everything disappeared, and it was just the two of us.

After a beautiful ceremony, Jack became my husband, and I became his wife.

JANUARY 3rd

Today marks the one-year anniversary of *Searching for the Truth: An Expedition into the Monster World* going on air. It might only be in its infancy, but it has become one of the more popular shows on the network with the episode featuring my boys as the most watched one. I have been working with Jack as his researcher, seeing which monsters we should be "hunting" for next. I also made sure we got those damn walkies among some other important equipment for our journeys.

Of course, today, as I was sifting through a plethora of articles to find our next monster, I noticed a headline that caught my eye:

"Strange Beings Are Seen in Lake Minnetaha and Surrounding Areas"

I called Jack over, "Hey, babe. Come check this out."

He came over and read it with me. It was about how some massive, odd-looking creatures, standing on two legs were being seen near Lake Minnetaha, Washington and neighboring towns. The furthest they've been seen is where Dr. Park's office is. It even mentioned Jack's show; how we were the first to capture them on film. I looked at him and said, "I want to go back and see them Jack, but with this article, do you think it might become unsafe?"

"It might. I'm actually surprised they got noticed. Unless..." we looked at each other, eyes widened with fear, "unless it's those other creatures they talked about."

"It has to be because the article mentions people getting attacked and property being damaged. They would never do that." Then I realized something that frightened me to my core. "Oh, god, babe, what if Nash, Cillian, or another creature got to them? What if they're hurt?"

Jack gently grabbed my shoulder. "I'm sure they're fine, babe. Look, even though we might've finished filming for season two, I'm going to contact the executives at the network and see if we can squeeze in another episode. A 'revisit' of our most popular one, that way we can get out there as soon as possible and check on them."

I relaxed a bit. "Yeah, that's not a bad idea. Thanks, babe."

"No problem. I'll call the execs now and see what they say."

"Sounds good." We kissed.

Until we get the "go ahead", I can at least continue to read up on them to make sure they're okay. The creatures are being dubbed "The Monsters of Lake Minnetaha".

Huh, not a bad name for a title!

Acknowledgements

It has taken me a little over a decade to live my dream of publishing my own work, but here it is! As selfish and conceited as this may sound, I am extremely proud of myself for being able to do this. There were several panic attacks and moments of uncertainty as I worked on it, but those are now being trumped by moments of joy and proudness. However, this wouldn't be happening if it wasn't for the help and support of some of the most amazing people in my life.

First, to my mom, Connie, and my brother, Anthony. You two have been by my side since, literally, day one. I cannot thank you both enough for your continued love and support. And thank you for believing in me.

To my entire family – my in-laws, my aunts, my cousins, and my nephews. Thank you for always cheering me on and supporting me.

To the "family I chose", my friends. Thank you for your constant love and support. I love you all more than you can ever understand.

To my beta readers: Erin Doherty, Paul Dickinson Russell, Meg Castro, Louise Stahl, Walter Cummins, Matt Giorgio, and Felicia Barash. (Hopefully, I'm not forgetting somebody and if I am, please forgive me!) You all took time out of your crazy, hectic days to read my story and tell me what was working and what wasn't. I cannot thank you enough for that! I especially want to give a shout out to Paul, Meg, and Felicia because if it wasn't for you three really scrutinizing my work and telling me what's missing in the plot, I don't think this story would've grown to what it is today. Thank you!

To my dear friend, "Uncle" Mark Bailey. Thank you *so* much for the incredible cover! I asked for red eyes and a scary looking title and you gave me a cover that I dreamed of, but never thought it would come true. Thank you, my fellow Godzilla fanatic!

To my angels up in heaven: Nanny, Poppy, Valarie, Angela, and my father, George. I love you all and miss you so much. I hope I have made you proud!

Lastly, to my amazing husband, John. Any person who found out their partner wanted to be a published author would possibly run away and say, "Well, you're a lost cause." However, you didn't! You stayed by my side, cheered me on, supported me, and pushed me every step of the way. Without you by my side, I have no clue where I would be at this moment, but I know I wouldn't be this happy. I love you so much! Thank you!

About the Author – Lisa Hodorovych

Writing has always been a constant for Lisa. Ever since she was little, she knew she was going to be an author and now, she's living her dream.

When she's not working on her own writing, she's either working with others on their stories through her company, Quoth the Writer, L.L.C., or she's posting book reviews, tea reviews, or Godzilla discussions on her social media.

She currently lives in New Jersey with her husband, John. When she's not working at all, she's either watching her favorite movies or TV shows, reading, or spending time with her family, friends, and husband.

Facebook: @LisaHodorovych or @QuoththeWriter
Instagram: @thewriterslife87 or @quoththewriter18

Made in the USA
Middletown, DE
19 March 2022